GUILTY OBSESSIONS
SHILOH WALKER

ELLORA'S CAVE
ROMANTICA PUBLISHING

An Ellora's Cave Romantica Publication

www.ellorascave.com

Guilty Obsessions

ISBN 9781419960277
ALL RIGHTS RESERVED.
Every Last Fantasy © 2004 Shiloh Walker
Guilty Needs Copyright © 2008 Shiloh Walker
Edited by Pamela Campbell.
Cover art by Syneca.

This book printed in the U.S.A. by Jasmine-Jade Enterprises, LLC.

Trade paperback Publication December 2009

With the exception of quotes used in reviews, this book may not be reproduced or used in whole or in part by any means existing without written permission from the publisher, Ellora's Cave Publishing, Inc.® 1056 Home Avenue, Akron OH 44310-3502.

Warning: The unauthorized reproduction or distribution of this copyrighted work is illegal. Criminal copyright infringement, including infringement without monetary gain, is investigated by the FBI and is punishable by up to 5 years in federal prison and a fine of $250,000.
(http://www.fbi.gov/ipr/)

This book is a work of fiction and any resemblance to persons, living or dead, or places, events or locales is purely coincidental. The characters are productions of the author's imagination and used fictitiously.

GUILTY OBSESSIONS
Shiloh Walker

ೞ

EVERY LAST FANTASY
~7~

GUILTY NEEDS
~77~

EVERY LAST FANTASY
☙

Author's Note

In this story, the heroine receives letters and email from an unknown man. Letters that, because of a past life connection, drive her to act in a way foreign to her. Now, in real life, we know courting this kind of behavior isn't safe...but this isn't real life. This is fantasy...enjoy.

Trademarks Acknowledgement

The author acknowledges the trademarked status and trademark owners of the following wordmarks mentioned in this work of fiction:

Mason Jars: Restaurant Specialties, Inc.

Disney World: Disney Enterprises, Inc.

Yahoo IM: Yahoo! Inc.

Every Last Fantasy

Prologue
London, 1840

With her back to the wall, Elaina tried to pretend as though she wasn't there. This just was not helping the way she had intended.

Yes, she was no longer suffering from the intense ennui that had plagued her since Richard's death. But the depression had only deepened. How could it do otherwise? Especially considering where she was. All this place did was remind her of how lonesome and empty she was.

"Whatever am I doing here?"

Elaina pressed a gloved hand to her temple as she tried to block out the unmistakable noises around her. A soft little voice in her head whispered, *Trying to get back to living, remember?*

Elaina had no use for living right now, no use for parties, no use for anything. Not since she had been forced to bury her husband years ago.

Her ennui wasn't natural—she knew this, but she couldn't get past it. No matter how hard she tried. No matter how lonely she was in the night. She couldn't find it in her to start trying to live again.

Finally, she had received Mary's invitation, and agreed to come to one of Mary's infamous parties.

Well, infamous in certain circles.

The parties had never been one of her favorite pastimes, but she wasn't going to move past her ennui if she did not get involved in life again.

Now, as she moved in slow circles, keeping her eyes down, she tried to figure a delicate way to leave without offending the hostess. Not that Mary wouldn't know. She need only take one look at Elaina's sad eyes.

Her eyes flickered up at a familiar sound, the sound of a hand coming down hard and fast on naked flesh, and against her will, her belly tightened, an ache settling in her pussy as she watched the tableau before her, the man striking at the woman's flesh as she lay across his lap, her pink buttocks up for all the world to see.

As Elaina dragged her eyes away, they passed over an unfamiliar face. One got to know many of the people at parties such as these. It was a rather small world. The men and women who played these kinds of games all flocked together.

But she didn't know him.

Mary appeared at her side, chuckling under her breath at the rapt look in Elaina's eyes. "Delicious, isn't he?" Mary asked as they stared at him. "He's an American, *new* money. His name is Jacob Moriarty."

Oh, yes...delicious, Elaina had to admit.

He was clean shaven, unlike so many of the men there, letting her see the splendid glory of his face. His mouth looked both hard and extremely kissable. He had emerald green eyes, thick, rich brown hair drawn back from his face in a short queue, much longer than the hairstyles of the men around him.

Jacob Moriarty was standing to the side, watching everything around him with faint amusement in his eyes. None of the little gatherings appeared to be catching his attention, no matter how many women slid their eyes his way. Of course, with all the naked bodies, chances were the eyes were the last thing a man would look at.

Mary chuckled and tapped Elaina's arm with her fan, ducking her head to murmur, "Perhaps I should introduce you?"

Every Last Fantasy

Elaina jerked her eyes away before the American could catch her staring at him. "No, no, please do not," Elaina whispered, shaking her head, but Mary was already moving away.

The look of him was imprinted on her mind. A shade above average height, but with broad shoulders, powerful arms, corded thighs that she could admire under the tight fit of his breeches. *My*...she thought as she touched her tongue to her lip before moving out of the room.

Elaina wished vainly she hadn't come. Group sex had simply never been her thing, even after Richard had introduced her to a more...*exciting* manner of sexual relations. But the sounds of all the passionate cries, watching the gleam of damp flesh under the flickering candlelight, tied her belly into hungry little knots, and her cleft wept with want.

Frustrated, tired and so achingly lonely, she pressed her lips together as she moved away from the party, slipping through the hall, studiously ignoring the woman who had gone to her knees before one man, suckling on the rigid stalk of his cock while another man lightly slapped at the pink cheeks of her ass with a riding crop.

"Do you wish for me to ride you, Elizabeth?" the man in front of her asked softly. "Shall I come in your throat...or in your silken little pussy?"

The words echoed in Elaina's head, reminiscent of similar experiences, years ago, with Richard. The memories brought tears to her eyes as need ate a hot little hole in her belly and Elaina suppressed a whimper as she ducked through a doorway and found herself in a silent and thankfully empty room. As she threw her handbag and her shawl down, she caught sight of her flushed face in the mirror, her breasts heaving above the gleaming gold lace of her bodice. Her womb ached.

She was so empty. With a cry, she tore at the laces of her gown. Gowns worn to a party such as this weren't the type you would wear anywhere else. All things were designed for quick undressing and dressing. In the heat of the moment, a lady did not want to bother with such things as a lady's maid.

As she finally fumbled enough buttons loose to remove the bodice, she sobbed in frustration, shoving it off, tearing at the ties at her waist and stepping loose of the thin material. No petticoat. If the proper ladies of London saw the way the women at such a party dressed, surely they would faint.

Standing before the mirror, she stared at her body, clad in the thin pantaloons, corset and chemise. The silk was so sheer, she could see the shadows between her thighs. Slowly, Elaina reached behind her, desperate to be free of the corset as well.

"Allow me," a soft voice behind her murmured.

She froze, her arms falling limply to her sides as she turned around.

Standing in the shadows by the door was the American whom Mary had pointed out to her, and he was staring at her with hot eyes and a wolfish smile.

"Do you not know how to knock, sir?" she demanded, lifting her chin imperiously.

He smiled. "You're so caught up in what you are doing, I doubt you would have heard." His eyes dropped to the low neckline of her chemise, a smile canting up the corner of his lips.

She shivered under his stare, feeling a fire she hadn't felt in years raging through her blood. As he lifted one hand and ran the back of his knuckles over the rounded upper slope of one breast, she felt cream soak the crotch of her pantaloons. "Sir…"

Lowering his head, he whispered quietly, "I have seen only one woman I wish to be with this evening. Had you accepted the offer of any of the men who had spoken to you tonight, I believe I would have gotten violent."

She licked her lips nervously. This was quite outrageous, she knew. But wasn't this exactly what she had wanted? A warm body, strong arms around her? Slowly, she turned around and presented him with her back, pulling her curls over her shoulder to allow him better access.

He stroked the shallow groove between her shoulder blades and murmured, "Not yet. I would like to see you in this, just this, for a few moments yet."

Elaina's limbs quivered as he caught her wrists and brought them together at the base of her spine. It was real silk he bound her with. She knew the different feel of rope, metal, cotton and silk. After he secured her wrists, she checked it slowly as he walked around her. Snug enough that she couldn't possibly work free, yet not so tight that it caused her any discomfort.

Her breath left her in a rush then as he fisted one hand in her hair and arched her mouth up to his.

*****

It had been three months since they had met. Three of the most wonderful months of her life.

Just tonight, he had asked her to marry him. She left with a smile on her face, floating out to the carriage and accepting the hand her coachman offered her, settling down in the padded seat as though it were made of clouds. She was quite certain she had never been this happy in her entire life.

With practiced hands, Elaina checked her hair, even though Jacob had helped her style it before she'd left. She stifled a giggle. He was a very accomplished lady's maid. How on earth he had learned such a skill, she didn't know. But that skill had proved very convenient over the past few months.

She sighed happily. After her husband had died two years earlier, she had been certain no other man would ever fill the void Richard had left in her life. Especially not the staid Baxter Lyles. No matter how her family tried to urge her into accepting his offer, she wouldn't. That man left her utterly cold.

Unlike Jacob... With a blissful sigh, she leaned back and closed her eyes, reliving the past hours.

Caught in her daydreams, she barely realized they had slowed to a stop until she heard the loud shout from outside the carriage. "Get on out of the road!"

Elaina shook her head, trying to clear the lust-induced fog of her memories from her mind. They couldn't possibly be home yet—why had they stopped? It took nearly an hour to travel to her townhouse—so why ever had they stopped?

Before she could even call out to Jim, though, there was a horrendous cracking sound, one so loud, she felt it within her soul. A gunshot. Fear, hot and thick, pooled in her belly and foreboding filled her as there was a thud from outside the carriage. Robbers?

But then the door swung open and she found herself staring into Baxter Lyles' face.

Every Last Fantasy

Chapter One
October

Oh, man… Vikky reached into the wooden crate, awe in her eyes. With gentle hands, she drew the old mirror from the packing material, shifting it so that the glass winked under the light. The surface wasn't perfectly smooth but it was so lovely, so different from anything she had ever owned. It made her think of hoopskirts, ladies' maids—so unbelievably feminine.

By far, this was the most wonderful treasure she had come ever across, as she'd gone through the things her aunt had left her.

Aunt Gloria had died nearly a year earlier but legalities and international nonsense had kept Vikky Morgan from receiving her inheritance for months. Finally, the lawyers notified her that the shop had been sold and she'd be receiving money from it shortly. In the meantime, there were a number of crates that had been packed up because her aunt had left specific instructions that they were to come to Vikky.

There had been a virtual treasure trove. Antique clothing meticulously cared for, jewelry from eras gone by, stick pins, earbobs, brooches and necklaces.

All of it most likely worth much more than this simple silver mirror.

But she felt as though she had been given the keys to the kingdom when she studied her reflection in the slightly uneven surface.

Vikky grinned widely, staring at her face.

Glancing back down into the crate, she saw a silver comb and something that looked like it would go in the hair, all set with a similar design to the mirror. Her eyes passed over the surface of the mirror as she set it down, then whipped back.

"What the hell?" she muttered.

For a moment, just the briefest second, there had been another face in the mirror. Similar to hers, but more delicate. The eyes were the same clear blue, and the same up-tilted nose. The only difference was the strawberry blonde curls piled on her head in an intricate knot, with one of the hair combs nestled just above one temple.

But she blinked and the image was gone.

Chapter Two

After the date from *hell*, Vikky stormed into her house and threw her purse on the couch.

Giving into the urge, she fisted her hands in the tumbled mass of her spiral curls and just screamed.

Why?

Why me?

Spinning around, she glared into the series of small mirrors that hung over her couch and stared at her image, reflected again and again. These loser jackasses wouldn't know how to handle a real woman with a guide and a pair of gloves.

Maybe she should write a manual, *The Dummy's Guide to Acting Like a Man*.

With a scowl, she muttered, "Maybe I should just give up on finding somebody."

And this last one had actually seemed so promising...well, according to Micky. *He's a cop, single, never been married...*

Yeah, and add jerk-off to the list. No wonder he's never been married. He can't talk to a woman without staring at her tits, she thought scathingly.

Flopping onto the couch, she stared up at the ceiling. Automatically, she reached out her hand and, by touch alone, found the mirror her aunt had left her. The thing belonged in a case, where it would be protected from dust, from age. But she couldn't stand that. She had to have it out where she could touch it, see it.

It usually stayed on the coffee table or her bedside table. It wasn't unusual for her to wake up holding it, having picked it up in her sleep.

Hugging it to her chest, she muttered, "Why can't I find somebody?"

All she wanted was a man who knew how to actually be a man, without being an asshole. You could find alphas who weren't total chauvinistic pigs, right? Or were they all gone?

That wasn't really asking too much, was it?

With a tired sigh, she turned onto her side and cuddled against the back of the couch, snagging the blanket and tugging it over her body. Against her breast, she held the mirror, cradling it like a teddy bear as a lone tear trickled out of one eye.

Geez, a real man…they had to still exist. Several of her friends were married to great guys.

So why couldn't she find one?

The twinkling lights of her Christmas tree reflected on the wall in the dim room and she just stared at it, blanking her mind, trying to lose herself in the beauty of the tree, the simplicity and joy of the season.

After a while, the lights of the tree, the scent of pine soothed her. And she felt warm, safe.

"It's Christmas," she told herself. "Don't let this drag you down."

She loved Christmas, always had. The way so many people seemed to have that warmth and giving spirit, the lights, the laughter and hope in the children's eyes…going to church with her parents and her friends, just taking joy in the beauty of it all. She cuddled around the mirror, which seemed oddly warm.

But damn it, it looked like she'd be spending Christmas alone.

Again.

*****

Vikky tried to drag her heels but Micky and Cindy were pulling on her hands insistently, grinning like loons as they forced her up to the dais where the man in the red suit sat waiting for them.

"C'mon...we'll all tell him what we want for Christmas, get a picture... It'll be *fun*," Cindy insisted, tugging hard when Vikky tried to balk. "You've done nothing but scowl most of the day. You need some fun."

Her face flushed red, while her soft blue eyes flickered for a brief moment as a thought passed through her mind. *What I want...*

Her disgust over the date from last night still hadn't faded.

Tell Santa what she wanted?

Oh, man... If she told the man in red what she wanted for Christmas, he just might have a heart attack. Old hearts just weren't intended for such shocks.

Of course, she was feeling evil enough that it just might improve her mood to cause a little bit of trouble. Snickering, she leaned over and whispered to Cindy, "I doubt he's ever had anybody tell him the things I could tell him."

Cocking her head, Cindy studied Vikky with shrewd hazel eyes. Then she grinned, a quick, wicked grin that lit her entire face. "You wouldn't dare," she whispered.

Vikky stopped right where she stood and said, "Wanna bet?"

Micky, already in line and paying, looked back at them. "What are you two up to?" she asked, rolling her eyes.

Vikky moved on past her friends, ignoring Micky as she flashed Cindy a wide grin and repeated, "Wanna bet?"

I'll be damned, Erik thought as the pretty, wide-eyed blonde sauntered closer to the gaily painted gilt chair he sat on.

Vikky Morgan…in the flesh. And what nice flesh it was. The little red sweater she wore hugged her small, pert little breasts and barely touched the top of her jeans. The jeans skimmed her hips like a second skin all the way down to her knees where they flared just slightly.

Her hair was still a wild mass of thick blonde curls, which she had scooped up into a ponytail, and the light of mischief danced in her pretty blue eyes.

After so many years of not seeing her, all of a sudden, there she was. And he had no doubt it was Vikky. Even when she had been a kid, that low husky laugh had bothered him.

Although, of course, it had been a little easier to put her out of his head when she was still a skinny little tomboy. Not anymore. She was long, sleek and sweetly curved in all the right places.

And he was going to see her, for the first time in years, wearing a red velvet Santa suit, fake beard, padded belly and all.

This was just perfect.

He recognized the two other ladies as Cindy Mertry and Mickayla Bishop. He'd seen Cindy a few times recently. She was his second cousin, although they had spent enough time together as kids that she felt like a kid sister. A very annoying, nosy, know-it-all kid sister. And he loved her as such, although he wouldn't tell her that.

Mickayla was an irritating twit, as far as he was concerned, more interested in forcing her opinions on others than understanding that other people had preferences of their own that were nothing like hers.

She'd been an obnoxious child, and even worse when she'd hit her teen years. She had been just the same when he had returned for his parents' funeral eight years ago. He had no doubt that she was still like that. As she edged between Cindy and Vikky, Erik grimaced.

What in the hell had he gotten into?

This was what happened when you agreed to do a favor for somebody, without finding out what the favor was first. He was going to hurt Morris Delaney for getting him into this, though. Oh, man, was he going to hurt him.

As Micky plopped her bony ass on his knee, he forced his mouth into a smile, and reminded himself that this was for a good cause. This particular mall always hired a Santa, just like any other, but the proceeds they received from it went to a kid's cancer hospital in Tennessee. So it was a good cause, even if he was having to listen to that annoying nasal twang as she drawled on about how she was looking for a new job, wanted to get out of the bank and expand her career horizons, but it had to come with a boss who wasn't a jerk, who'd let her have off the days she needed, and maybe somebody who'd let her get online at work.

Then she wanted a man, but she wanted one who wouldn't be too pushy with sex, because she really didn't...

"Ah, Miss? You know, these aren't usually the things you ask Santa for," he finally said. "You know, jewelry, a yacht..."

Micky laughed, the sound grating on his ears. "Well, I believe in the power of positive thinking — if I say it out loud, it helps it actually happen."

Cindy snorted. "Micky, darling, I love you, really. But there's not enough positive thinking in the world to get you what you want in life. You don't even know," she drawled, shaking her head. "Come on, it's my turn."

Cindy was easier. She just wanted to pass the upcoming finals. She was working on her Masters in nursing and she was as quick and sharp as they came. She would pass, no problem, and it wouldn't take any magic from a man in a Santa suit.

As Vikky came strolling up, a mischievous grin on her face, Erik felt his heart stutter. Oh, hell. He knew what the light in her eyes meant. She was up to something. Even when she was a kid, that light had meant trouble. And he seriously doubted that had changed since he'd last seen her.

He looked awfully young to be a Santa, Vikky mused as she lowered her butt onto his thigh. The length of leg under her bottom felt damned hard and the skin above his beard, around his eyes, was too smooth for him to be as old as the Santas usually were.

The gray-green eyes gleaming at her over his gold-rimmed, crescent shaped spectacles looked kind of familiar but nobody she knew would take time to work as a Santa in a mall. Even though this was one of the classiest Santa jobs known to man, with the real red velvet suit, the richly painted chair. Hell, most of the stodgy old men she knew from the bank were so damned uptight, they could eat coal and pop out diamonds.

His voice seemed a little strained as he said, "So what kind of Christmas wish do you have, young lady?"

Flicking Cindy a glance, she saw the dare in her eyes, watched as she shook her head. She didn't think she'd do it. After the weekend she'd just had, she sure as hell would. If for no other reason than to blow off some steam.

And at least he looked young enough for his heart to take it. Inching forward, she curled an arm around his shoulders, waggled her fingers at the camera and smiled before turning to look at Santa.

Lowering her head, she whispered...

"I want to be taken..."

And she was tired of playing alone. She whispered that into his ear in a voice that had dropped to a low murmur, one that sent shivers down his spine.

She had shocked the hell out of him and he suspected that was exactly why she had done it. He'd seen the glance shared between her and Cindy—*that* should have warned him. But no...

He asked, "Taken where? Disney World?"

And she laughed, a low, husky sound that tightened his flesh as she pressed a finger to her lips, hushing him.

"No, silly Santa. I want to be *taken*...by a man. I'm tired of men who don't know how to treat a woman, and I'm tired of being handled with kid gloves."

His cock pounded within the confines of the jeans he wore under the baggy red trousers. Shifting, he forced a pained smile and said, "I'll see what I can do."

Vikky liked it wild.

As she strolled away, she tossed her curls over her shoulder and winked at Santa, ignoring Cindy's giggles and Micky's repeated questions of, "What did you tell him?"

He still looked a little...un-Santalike. His eyes had flashed hot and maybe it was her imagination, but his body seemed to get hotter, the heat reaching out to her own body. *Well, that had been fun.*

And maybe, just maybe, whoever was in charge of granting wishes would be amused enough to let her have her wish.

But in the meantime, she had a Christmas bonus to burn.

As she strolled down the tiled walkway of the mall, her eyes lit on a purse in a window display. Delighted, she grabbed Cindy's hand and dragged her in, as Micky continued to ask, "What did you say?"

Vikky said, "I just told him what I wanted for Christmas." She shrugged as she eyed the purse in the window greedily. Catching the eye of the salesclerk, she pointed, arching an eyebrow and smiling as the lady nodded.

Cindy snorted. "She was a bad girl—she's not getting anything but coal and a spanking."

"Oooohhhh, do you really think I can have the spanking?" Vikky teased, wiggling her eyebrows suggestively.

"You are messed up," Micky said.

The saleslady suppressed a smile as she caught the tail end of the conversation. She gave the lady a quick wink before pasting an innocent expression on her face as she turned to face Micky. "Messed up? Why? Because I like to be spanked? I consider having sex with animals messed up. I'm just adventurous."

Then she turned, smiled gaily at the salesclerk who was now muffling a laugh as she held out the purse.

From the corner of her eye, she saw Micky's face turn fiery red with embarrassment as she realized they had been overheard.

Vikky ignored her and asked, "I don't suppose there is a wallet that goes with the purse, is there?"

Pasting a bland expression on her face, the salesclerk took the purse, her eyes dancing with amusement. "I believe there is..."

Twenty minutes later, she had a new purse and a new wallet and she walked out of the store with a wide grin. It faded as Micky marched up and hissed in her ear, "Do you *have* to do things like that?"

An old argument. Would Micky ever understand that just because something wasn't right for her didn't mean it wasn't right for somebody else? Would she ever stop making sour little comments and picking fights, then getting offended when the other person didn't back down?

Tired of it, Vikky stopped and met her friend's furious eyes levelly. "No. I don't. Do you have to criticize anything that isn't missionary sex? Grow up, Micky. Not everybody has the hang-ups about sex that you do," she said flatly, then she turned on her heel and stalked away, grumbling under her breath.

Behind her, Micky's jaw dropped and her eyes widened.

Every Last Fantasy

Cindy rolled her eyes. "Come off it, Mick. You two have been through this a thousand times. You tug Vikky's tail and you're not going to walk away without a scratch. Now come on, let's go to the steak place and order a margarita and flirt with the bartender."

Late that night, Erik tossed on the uncomfortable hotel bed.

He could have gone on into town but, since he had agreed to spend the weekend playing Santa, he didn't want to bother with driving an hour to and from Corydon.

His sleep was chaotic but, for once, he wasn't plagued by the images of Mike and Iraq. Instead, he dreamed of *her*. It wasn't an unfamiliar dream—he had been having it for a few weeks now but, as always, it made no sense at all. Usually, the dream bounced from them fucking, to them dancing, to him searching for her before being lost in darkness.

No sex this time. No searching either. All he could see the pretty woman with sunset-gold curls swept up away from her face. His heart clenched as she laughed up at him, her wide blue eyes dancing with amusement, bright with emotion. There was a gilt butterfly in her hair and her tits spilled over the edge of something lacy and exotic. Her long legs were covered in something silky, so sheer he could see the mound of her pussy through it.

Her eyes went from smiling and laughing to full of hunger and heat... Then everything shifted and he moaned in his sleep as her face became the ghostly outline of a skeleton's—eyes empty, mouth gaping open.

* * * * *

"So, do you think there's anything you can do?" Vikky had asked him, a teasing lilt to her voice, her pretty blue eyes dancing merrily.

Hell, yeah, he'd see what he could do.

As Erik pulled into the small Indiana town where they'd grown up, he recalled the Santa episode. That woman was dangerous. Oh, he figured she had done it just because Cindy had assumed she wouldn't—and maybe she did it to aggravate Mickayla.

But she had been speaking the honest truth, he suspected.

And damned if he hadn't been more turned on than he'd ever been in his life.

Drumming his fingers on his thigh, he debated whether or not to go into the bank and see if she was there. He almost pulled away.

Almost.

But then he recalled that low, husky laugh, that wicked gleam in her bluer-than-blue eyes and that odd, hopeful note to her voice.

He had felt more alive since talking to her than he had felt in months.

Oh, yeah. He was going in.

It was Monday and she was back at work. Her episode with Santa had passed and she had all but shoved it out of her mind. Good for a giggle at the time, but her mood had dropped again, swinging awfully low and she knew damn good and well that teasing some stranger wasn't going to do a damn thing for it this time.

She needed a change. A big change.

Ah hell, Vikky mused as Rosa Fielding continued to jaw on about her gout, and her bad heart, and her rheumatism. *I need to get laid.*

Bad.

She grimaced as she was finally able to get away from old Mrs. Fielding. With her back to the counter, she caught Micky's gaze and rolled her eyes, suppressing the urge to make a stabbing motion at her belly.

Every Last Fantasy

Kill me now, she mouthed.

Micky smirked.

Damn, that woman was as long-winded as they came. Her ears practically ached from listening to her gab for the past thirty minutes. She shot hopeful glance at the clock and saw that she only had about ten minutes to go until lunch. *Eureka...a break!*

From the corner of her eye, she saw a large shadow step up to her window and she plastered a bright, friendly smile on her face. Those eyes...

That was the first thing she noticed, his eyes. Big gray-green eyes with thick lashes. Then he smiled, a slight lift to one corner of his mouth.

"I don't believe it...Erik Fortner," she said, shaking her head and leaning on the counter, staring at him with a dopey grin.

Damn, he was still as good-looking as he had been ten years ago.

"Hello, Vikky," he said. The low, rough voice sent a shiver down her spine, rubbing over her skin like a caress.

"What are you doing back in Corydon? Aren't you a big-time hotshot reporter now?" she drawled.

He laughed, leaning his elbows on the counter. "I'm not a reporter. I'm a photojournalist...big difference," he said. "And I'm taking a break. A very long one."

She watched something dark and grim enter his eyes and her heart went out to him. "I heard you spent some time over in Iraq. I'm awfully glad to see you're still in one piece," she said quietly.

He shrugged. "That's why I'm taking the break. My head...some of the things I saw are messing with my mind. I think it was the right thing, going over there, but still... My mind is raw from it," he said, his eyes taking on a far-off look. For a second, she thought he forgot where he was, and when he blinked and looked around, a bemused look in his eyes, it just helped confirm that idea.

"It's really good to see you, Erik," she said, smiling, leaning over to peck his cheek across the counter.

He turned his head and she could almost swear he did it on purpose so, at the last second, her lips brushed his mouth instead of his cheek. And her entire body literally sizzled from that light contact. Pulling back, she felt the blood rushing to her face as he said, "Oops. Sorry."

Judging by the look in his eyes, he wasn't sorry at all.

Licking her lips, she tried to find something to fill that sudden silence but, before she had really even started to think, he asked, "When is your lunch? This place still close for an hour?"

She chuckled. "This is small town America, Erik. Of course we close for lunch. The CEO tried to change that but then the ladies caught wind of it and had a talk with his wife, so it was a no-go."

"Why don't you let me take you to lunch then?"

Thirty minutes later, she was shifting in her seat and wondering if she had lost her mind. Unless she was sorely mistaken, Erik was hitting on her. And very hard. But in a way so subtle, she couldn't really put her finger on it.

His hand brushed against hers, he pulled out her chair and scooted his around on the pretext of not wanting to yell to talk to her, he reached over to brush her hair out of her eyes and his hand lingered.

Her belly jumped, jittered, tightened. It felt hot and achy, and her pussy all but wept with need as she shifted and squirmed on the chair.

In short, she was more turned on just from having lunch with him than she had been all year. As he leaned forward, she could feel the whisper of his breath on her face, her neck. She hoped to hell she wasn't blushing as she felt her nipples tighten under the lace and silk of her bra.

"So have you got any plans for Christmas?"

Vikky shrugged, lifting one shoulder absently as she stabbed at her salad with her fork. "I don't know… Not really, I guess. Going to my mom's for a while. I usually love Christmas, but this year…it's just kind— I dunno. I feel kinda blah."

Erik sighed. "I can understand that." A wildfire grin lit his face as he asked, "You just need something special for a Christmas present. Anything you'd like?"

Something about the way he asked, or maybe it was that innocent look in his amazing eyes, but all she could think of at that moment was when she'd whispered her wishes to the Santa. Her face flamed as her heart seemed to swell within her chest, slamming against her rib cage.

Swallowing, she dropped her eyes to the table and mumbled, "No. Not really."

"Awww, c'mon. Everybody wants *something* for Christmas."

Oh, yeah, like she was going tell *him*. Tell him about that wish, the same wish she'd wanted for years, since her last boyfriend had up and decided he didn't want some freak bitch who liked being spanked, or liked being held down while he fucked her. Forcing a shrug, she lied, "I haven't really thought about it."

Oh, yes she had.

Her face flushed the cutest damned shade of pink just then. Erik fought the urge to scoop her onto his lap and cuddle her. She was so obviously flustered—and turned on. He could see it in the way she kept shifting on her chair, in the fast pace of her breath, the tell-tale rush of blood to her face.

Damn, he wanted a bite of her. A banquet.

And something told him she would be more than amenable to the idea. If he could just figure out how to handle it.

But this wasn't the time or the place. And if he kept teasing her like this, kept seeing that sweet flush, her nervous laughter, he was going to explode.

So he steered the conversation to easier ground while, in the back of his mind, he plotted.

Erik pressed his face into the pillow, caught in a dream he couldn't escape. No pretty lady this time, and no skeleton faces gazed at him with empty eyes.

Damn it, he couldn't go back…couldn't… *Mike!*

In the dream, he was caught staring at the video, over and over, watching as Mike's body fell lifeless to the ground. *Shoulda tried harder to get us out of there, buddy. I'm so sorry…*

The sound of his own hoarse voice still echoed through the air as he jerked himself awake. Sitting up in the bed, he stared with dull horror at the wall in front of him, reliving the moment of Mike's death. At least it had been quick, not as brutal as so many he had seen and heard of over the past months. Just a single shot through the heart, from the back. Mike hadn't even known it was coming.

Small miracle.

They had been forced to hide, worried that they would be the next innocents plucked from their beds at night, woken from a sound sleep by gun-wielding guerillas, as had happened to so many others. No. It had been their last week, time to go home, and all Mike had been doing was walking down the street.

He had been cut down by gunfire as an explosion sounded from the street behind them. Another building blown up, more innocent bystanders killed.

If Amad hadn't dragged Erik out of there, he probably would have been the next lifeless corpse lying in the street.

But, even though they had to have heard his screams, no one came looking for them. Amad had pulled him away, kicking and bellowing, tears streaming from his eyes until finally the tall, quiet man had done something that made black dots dance in front of Erik's eyes.

When he awoke, he had a splitting headache and a hole in his heart.

He was also en route back to America. Amad had stared at him from across the cabin of the jet and said quietly, "I am sorry, my friend. But I will not see another friend of mine die there. As much as I value what you and Michael set out to do, I will not allow you to remain."

Part of him had wanted to argue.

But the other part of him had just been…tired.

Now, weeks later, he still didn't feel much better. He had no desire to return to Iraq, although several magazines had offered handsome sums of money.

Hell, what good is the money if I don't live to spend it? At one time, it wouldn't have mattered, money or no. Erik would have gone for the thrill, the adventure, the adrenaline rush.

There was no thrill now, no adventure. And the adrenaline rush had come too many times from watching people die under the hands of zealots, the taste of fear and anger ripe in his mouth.

Grimly, Erik shoved the memories aside, trying to push them out of his mind as he swung his legs out of bed and pushed to his feet, his belly hot and tight, grief knotting his throat.

He had seen too much death, way too much death. So walking away had been easy.

It was sleeping at night that was hard.

* * * * *

Vikky flopped onto her belly, humming softly as she danced in her sleep around and around a grand ballroom, her hair swept up off her shoulders, spilling down in a riot of fat curls. Warm, strong arms cradled her against a broad chest and part of her felt scandalized—*a man shouldn't hold a woman so close while dancing!*

Oh, but she liked it. Quite a bit. Just as she loved the way his chest pressed against her bosom, the way she could feel his legs through the silk of her gown and the layers of petticoats. One thigh moving between hers as they danced, holding her so close that from, time to time, she rode the muscled length between her thighs.

The dream shifted and she was all but nude, wearing only her corset over a pair of sheer pantaloons, blushing as she looked down and saw the pink of her nipples over the edge of her corset. It bit ever so slightly into her flesh, since he had told her not to wear a chemise under it.

He walked into the room and she lifted her eyes, staring up at him from her kneeling position on the floor, feeling heat spark in her pussy as his eyes ran over her bound form, her hands tied together behind her back and then fastened to her ankles.

Her belly clenched as she watched his hands go to his breeches. Her mouth watered as she watched him free his cock, her mind whirled. Would he spank her again? Hold her head as he thrust his cock inside her mouth?

Oh, she loved that, how he would force his length inside her mouth, as she knelt bound and waiting at his feet.

Or would he just take her? Drop to his knees behind her and fuck her hard and rough, withholding her climax until she begged him to let her come.

Her tongue darted out to wet her lips as she stared at him, her gaze dropping to the ruddy length of his cock as he moved toward her. But before he did anything else, the dream fell apart once more, reforming... Caught! Trapped...couldn't breathe...so cold...

Vikky awoke gagging and gasping for air. Tumbling out of the bed, she ran into the bathroom and puked into the toilet, vomiting up what looked like...*water*?

Chapter Three

Erik eyed the note and almost threw it away.

Damn it, he didn't need to do this. He could just ask her out.

But then he remembered the light in her eyes, the yearning, dreamy look, and the underlying knowledge that she was wasting her time.

That woman didn't look like she'd had fun for a long time. *Come to think of it*, Erik mused, *neither have I.*

Hell. He could give it to her, see what happened. And if she wasn't as…adventuresome as she liked to think, he could call the game off. No harm, no foul. *Fair, right?*

It was the *life* that surged through him that made up his mind. He hadn't felt alive in months, even before Mike's death. The months he had spent in Iraq had killed something inside of him. Or he had thought it had. Until now. Looking at her made him feel alive again.

Granted, ever since seeing her again, these dreams of his had become even more vivid—so vivid they were intruding on his waking hours. Dreams where he wore clothing that looked like it belonged in the set of *A Christmas Carol*, where he alternately danced, teased and fucked a woman who looked suspiciously like Vikky.

Her name was Elaina.

His mind was overcrowded by images of him tying her down, legs spread, arms over her head as he sprawled between her thighs, feasting on her pussy, listening as she moaned and pleaded. Images of him spanking a slim, rounded little ass as he fucked his way into her pussy, her hands bound at the base of her spine.

A car horn blared from down the street, jerking him out of his reverie. His cock throbbed in his jeans as he shook his head, shoving the remnants of the most recent dream away. He looked back to the note, rubbing it with his thumb as fire flowed through his veins.

Setting his jaw, Erik made his way up to her house, glancing around to make sure he didn't have an audience.

He'd just see what came of it.

That was it.

* * * * *

Vikky stared at the heavy vellum in her hand, entranced.

What in the hell?

It read, simply: *All I want for Christmas is…you.*

Looking around, she searched the yard but there was nobody there who didn't belong.

Vividly, she remembered her wish to Santa.

Oh, man. Knowing her luck, that guy was a sicko and he had followed her home.

Hell, that was ridiculous. He was harmless. She was delusional. She was paranoid…

And she was about as turned on as she had ever been in her life.

From a *note*. Just a note.

But who in the hell had it come from?

Maybe somebody had seen him.

Anyone who showed up here would be noticed by a hundred busybodies. If somebody who didn't belong in town was here, everybody would have known five seconds after it happened. Glancing around with a frown, she debated going to Ms. Westmore's house and asking her. If she did, and the woman suspected something was up, Vikky would never get out of there.

Besides... It was kinda...cool.

Tucking her woolen cloak around her body more closely, she headed back inside, still staring at the paper. She sat down on the couch, drawing her knees to her chest, unaware that she was once more reaching for her mirror, cradling it against her chest as she stared at the note in bemusement.

Wondering.

* * * * *

She was even more intrigued, and a little nervous, when another note appeared on her door the next day.

Have you been a good girl, Vikky? I kind of hope not.

And there was a rather weird jumble of letters and numbers down at the bottom. *Exxiled010.*

Frowning, Vikky rubbed her thumb over them as she went inside. She dropped onto the couch, as was her habit, looking at the note. For some odd reason, she kept remembering her dream from last night, how she had danced with a man more handsome than anybody she'd ever met in her life. Dancing first in an exquisite ball gown, and then in nothing at all as her partner lowered his head to murmur in her ear, *Have you been good while I was away?*

With a monumental effort of will, she shoved the memory of the dream away. She lifted the mirror and stilled as it caught the reflection of her computer over in the corner. It shouldn't have. Wrong angle. But she was staring right at it. The mirror was in her lap, below the back of the couch. The computer was at her desk, to the right, far back against the wall.

She licked her lips as she closed her eyes. *I think I'm losing my mind,* she thought as she opened them. Now in the mirror, she saw only her face. Slowly, she turned her head and looked at the computer's blank screen as she quoted part of the note aloud in a soft, shaky voice, "Exxiled010."

Rising, she walked toward the computer. Halfway, she stopped and walked back, forcibly setting her mirror down. That mirror was becoming a security blanket for her. If she was in the house, she couldn't go five minutes without touching it. *Just a mirror, for crying out loud*, she told herself as she stalked over to the computer and dropped into her chair.

Booting up the computer, she waited until the yellow smiley face from the IM program opened his eyes with a smile, signaling that she was now logged into the network.

She ignored the different pop-ups that appeared as she entered the command for an IM to somebody not on her list. The box opened and she tapped in *Exxiled010*, adding a simple, *Hello?*

Immediately, the message that somebody was sending a response appeared. *Aren't you fast, sugar?*

Eureka. That was the first thought that went through her brain. And then nerves arced through her. Vikky froze, almost terrified, but the curiosity was eating a hole in her belly. *Do I know you?*

Do you want to? he responded easily.

Yes! resounded through her entire soul but her head was a little more cautious than her libido. *Cute, slick. Very cute. But not the answer I was aiming for.*

Vikky, you know me as well as I know you...and, might I add, I'd love to see how that red lipstick you like to wear would look on me – one place in particular.

Cream flooded her pussy. Just as simply as that, in one blunt, evocative statement. She was so turned on, she couldn't think straight. With nervous, shaking hands, she typed, *You are a shy one, aren't you?*

Shy isn't what you are looking for, Vikky. Tell me something... What did it make you feel like? What I just said?

Vikky sank her teeth into her lip, reclining back into the chair, the blood pounding hot and heavy inside her veins. She needed to get up. Walk away from the computer, maybe call the police. This guy knew who she was. Where she lived.

Logically, she knew this.

So it came as a bit of a surprise when she saw herself tapping out a response.

Hot.

Silence for a long moment. Then the question, *Are you wet?*

Yes.

He responded with, *Good. Keep your eyes on the screen but sit back, slide your hand inside your panties...touch yourself. I want to think about you playing with yourself until you come. And know that, sometime very soon, I'm going to be touching you.*

Some of her normal personality reasserted itself, rearing its head as a droll smile appeared on her face. She tapped out, *<snort> You're awfully sure of yourself, slick.*

I didn't say you could do anything but touch yourself. Now do it.

The heat hit her belly like a fist—sudden, air-stealing and powerful. And Vikky leaned back, her body shivering, her nipples tight and aching. Still staring at the screen, she slid her fingers inside her panties and started to circle the throbbing bud of her clit.

She whimpered as she touched herself, her fingers slid slickly over her wet, swollen clit, plunged inside her pussy, hard and fast, as she stared ahead with blind, unseeing eyes.

A tiny chime sounded and she forced her heavy-lidded eyes back to the screen, sinking her teeth into her lip to keep from crying out as she read the message.

You're touching yourself now...aren't you? Don't answer. I already know. Are you wet? Hot? Are your nipples aching?

Unconsciously, she answered him aloud. "Yes..."

I ache. I want to spread you out on my bed, spank that pretty little ass of yours until it turns pink, then I want to fuck you until you scream for mercy. Make yourself come... I'm imagining feeling you around me and I want to know you're coming while I do it.

The orgasm was the most powerful she'd had in months...years. With quick, hard thrusts of her fingers, she rode it to the very end, sobbing and panting.

And when it was over, she was left staring at the little IM box with wide, disbelieving eyes.

She was out of her head.

On the other side of town, Erik pumped his hand up and down the length of his cock, head back, eyes slitted as he stared at the computer.

She was touching herself, sliding her fingers around the hard little bud of her clit, maybe pumping them in and out... She'd be moaning now, then sinking her teeth into her lip to muffle her screams...

Oh, yeah.

He could see it all too clearly in his mind's eye. How she looked as she came, the soft strangled cries that fell from her lips, how she trembled as she pumped her hips, her strawberry blonde curls clinging to her face and neck.

Strawberry blonde? Damn it, she had golden curls. Vikky's hair was like liquid gold, not strawberry blonde.

His cock jerked in his hand and he hissed as he felt the climax building inside him. Next time... Next time he was going to be pumping inside the hot creamy depths of her pussy.

The orgasm took him by surprise with its intensity. Thrusting up off the chair, he groaned, the tendons in his neck standing out as he arched his head back, hot spurts of seed splashing onto his belly, coating his hand as he pumped himself dry.

Damn.

He really had to get her into bed. Either her, or this crazy dream creature who plagued his nights.

* * * * *

Erik watched as she left the bank, the wind whipping the long black skirt around her legs. She glanced around as she dug out her keys and he grinned. "Are you looking for me, sugar?" he whispered to himself.

Well, she was getting ready to find him.

In a way.

After a week of messages and IM's, Erik had come to the conclusion that she had definitely been honest when she'd told Santa she wanted to be taken. And he had come to the conclusion that he had to have her. Vikky and the dream woman had merged and tangled inside his mind until they were one to him.

He hadn't seen a woman so ready to be fucked in a long while.

And he was going to do it, damn it.

Erik kept a few cars between them as he followed her home and then, as she pulled into the driveway, he drove past. The house he was renting was on the street right behind hers. How convenient.

As he waited for night to fall, he paced, nerves and anticipation brewing inside of him until he thought he'd jump out of his skin.

Control, he told himself.

He needed to get control.

Vikky found herself battling back disappointment when there was no note on her door. And no message waiting on the IM for her, either.

Every Last Fantasy

She refused to admit she was sulking as she flopped onto the couch, staring at the TV without really seeing it. Her fingers itched but she refused to pick up the mirror. She felt cold without it. *Could you get addicted to a mirror?*

For crying out loud, it was ridiculous to get this upset because some guy she didn't even know wasn't flirting with her today.

But the thing was...she *felt* like she knew him. He was teasing her off and on and there was something almost familiar about it. Like — well, like she knew him. And she felt as though he knew her. He knew what kind of candy she ate at the movies, and knew her dad had died years ago.

Knew that she was dying for a chance to experience some of the things she had only dreamed about. How some of the things he told her echoed dreams and fantasies of her own, like dancing with her while she wore a dress that was gold and lacy, then peeling it off of her piece by piece as they danced until she was fully nude, and he was still clothed.

How did he know that?

Even if he did know her.

How?

Lowering her mug of tea to the table, she reached for the remote, cocking her head and listening. Light danced on the surface of the mirror but she closed her hand into a fist and didn't pick it up.

She heard something outside.

Shivering, she stood, folding her arms around herself as paranoia started to set in. She shouldn't have told that Santa wanna-be about her dreams. Shouldn't have gotten so aroused by those short little notes, those late night chats.

Opening the door, Vikky stared outside, inching forward just a little as she tried to see beyond the small circle of light that spilled out of the open door. She inched herself to the edge of the concrete patio at her back door, searching the darkness for whatever she had heard.

When the big warm hands came up to rest on her shoulders, she jumped, a scream building inside her throat.

"Hey, sugar," a soft, rough voice whispered in her ear as he wrapped his arms around her and kept her from turning around.

Inexplicably, the fear that had flooded her drained away at those words. Unreasonable, illogical, but, while her head tried to tell her that she didn't know what he was up to, her body was already ignoring her and listening to him.

"You," she whispered, her voice shaking as he lowered his head and kissed her neck. From the corner of her eye, she saw a glimpse of hair — thick and pale in the light.

Chuckling, he nuzzled her hair as he cupped her hips in his hands and pulled her back against him. She fought not to whimper as she felt the hard length of his cock through their layers of clothing.

"Who are you?" she whispered.

"Somebody who is going to give you every last fantasy you've ever had," he murmured.

She laughed nervously, trying to pull away from his hands. "All of them?"

He stopped her movements by simply wrapping his arms completely around her and pinning her against him. "Yes...all of them. Starting now. Close your eyes," he purred. Shivering, she stood still as she felt something warm and fuzzy on her face, then covering her eyes.

Her heart slammed against her rib cage as he turned her around. He was staring at her now, she could feel it, but, behind the blindfold, her eyes were useless. She couldn't see anything. His hands came up to cup her face and her skin was unbelievably sensitive as he slid his fingers into her hair, the rough, hard skin of his palms against her cheeks.

Vikky whimpered as he covered her mouth with his, his tongue pushing boldly into her mouth, taking, claiming... His hands skimmed down her back and her heart stuttered as he cupped her ass and lifted her.

His cock, covered by a thick layer of denim, seemed to burn through his clothing and hers, imprinting on her belly. With a hungry moan, Vikky arched against him.

She felt them moving, then the wall at her back as he pinned her against it. "Are you scared?" he asked, pulling his mouth away.

"Ummm, yes." she squeaked out. *Terrified.* And if he stopped, she was going to kill him.

"Good," he chuckled. He tore her skirt away.

Chapter Four

Blood rushed to her face as Erik stared down at the smooth pale oval, her mouth trembling, her tongue darting out to wet her lips. The blindfold fit snugly over her eyes, keeping her from seeing him. The downside, it also kept him from watching her eyes as he took her.

Lowering his head, he whispered into her ear, "I've been dying to know, but didn't want to ask. Do you shave? Wax? Go natural? I wanted to see for myself. I've been going out of my mind, dying to see your pussy."

A shuddering gasp left her as he lifted his head. Her cheeks were flaming and, as he watched, she started to chew on her lower lip. Moving back, he kept his eyes on her face as he ran his hand down the front of her body, between her breasts, across her belly, past the hem of the short, snugly fitted sweater, to slide his fingertips along the waistband of her panties.

Teasing them both, he followed the line of her panties around to the back, smiling as it dipped down between the cheeks of her ass. Damn, he loved seeing a woman in a thong. He gripped the swatch of material and tugged, watching as her lips parted and a soft moan slipped from her.

"Like that?" he asked, releasing his hold on her panties and sinking to his knees in front of her.

She whimpered and rocked her hips back and forth, a hungry little female gesture that drove him nuts. Damn it, he hurt. His cock was so hard he thought he was going to explode.

Erik slid her panties down her thighs, taking them down with firm pressure as he glided his hands over the sleek length of her legs. He stared up into her face, waiting until he slid the panties completely off before he dropped his eyes to her sex. "You wax, don't ya, sugar?" he whispered, running the backs of his knuckles over the smooth lips of her pussy. A trim little patch of hair sat right on her pubis and the flesh of her mound felt soft, smooth...and wet. Cupping her cleft in his hand, he whispered, "You're so hot, so wet. You like having somebody blindfold you, tear your clothes off. I know it's cold out here but you don't really even seem to notice. And people might see... Does that bother you?"

"Yes...no...damn it, I don't know... Please," she said, her voice coming in broken little stops and starts.

He laughed softly at her answer, at the nerves evident in her voice, the nerves and the arousal, heaven help him, the sheer curiosity. "Ever been fucked in public, Vikky?" he whispered.

"No," she breathed. Then her mouth curved into a cheeky smile as she added, "At least, not yet."

With a wicked grin, he whispered, "Too bad it's so damn cold. Of course, you're so hot, you could warm us both all winter long."

He rose and reached for the doorknob, shoving the door open before he picked her up. One of her hands went to his shoulder but the other started to reach for the blindfold. "Don't touch it, Vikky."

Her hand fell away as he carried her inside, lowering her to the floor beside the kitchen table, bending his head to buss her lips. "I've things I want to do to you," he murmured, walking around her, staring at her as she stood there, wearing nothing but a red sweater, a blush and a pair of black boots that went up to her knees.

He stopped behind her, just to the side, caressing the taut, trembling skin of her ass. "Do you have a problem with that?" he asked gently, right before he lifted his hand and smacked her ass—a sharp, stinging little slap.

When the harsh, hungry cry fell from her lips, Erik could have screamed out in triumph. She hadn't been just running that sassy little mouth of hers. She wanted exactly what he wanted to give her.

"Take your sweater off," he ordered gruffly. "I want to see those pretty little breasts."

She did so, her motions slow, hesitant. "The bra, too." As the lace and silk fell away, her hands clenched reflexively and her arms started to move. "Don't cover up, baby. I want to see you, all of you, before I fuck you."

Damn, she was perfect. Long and slim with high, firm little tits, crowned with dark pink nipples that he was just dying to bite. He walked around her, making sure his boot heels were loud enough that she could hear him moving. She stood still but he could hear the rapid pace of her breathing. There was a flush of arousal climbing up her torso, from her pretty little breasts to her face. He cupped one taut, firm ass cheek in his hand, humming with approval.

"Pretty ass, pretty tits...pretty everything, Vikky, and damn, I want a bite," he teased, watching as her mouth parted and her tongue slid out to wet her lips. "You like hearing that?" he asked.

She nodded wordlessly, one hand lifting, reaching out to him, then she stopped and let her hand fall back to her side.

"Good," he purred. "Because I have all sorts of things I want to do to you, tell you... So many ways I want to fuck you."

Guiding her around, he moved her until she stood just at the table. Placing her hands on it, he whispered, "Bend over. I want to see you bent over and waiting for me. I'm going to spank that pretty little butt of yours."

"Oh, man," she moaned. She bent over until her pert, round ass was lifted and waiting.

He slapped one cheek, then the other, listening when she cried out—broken little pleas and moans—as he slapped lightly at the taut flesh. "You like being spanked, baby. Damn, listen to you moan." He stopped, moved back, watched as she rocked her hips against the table, as though riding a man. The pink flesh of her pussy was open and glistening wetly. His cock jerked, demanding that he fuck her — fuck her *now*.

Licking his finger, he pressed it against the tight, pink pucker of her ass, smiling as her body shivered and she keened low in her throat. "Hmmm, you like that, don't you?" he murmured, smacking lightly at her ass.

When she didn't answer with anything more than another moan, he spanked her again, harder, feeling hot lust tear through him as she shuddered. "You like it? Tell me or I'll stop."

"Don't stop!" she cried, shoving her butt back against him. "Yeah, I like it... Please don't stop."

Slowly, he pushed against the tight muscle, resting his other hand low on her spine, his balls drawing tightly against his body as the silken, snug flesh of her bottom clutched at his finger. He worked it inside with slow, certain pressure. "You've been fucked in the ass before?"

Again, she didn't offer much of an answer beyond those hungry little moans. As much as he liked the sound of them, he wanted more. With another resounding smack on her ass, he said, "Have you?"

She cried out and he watched as her knuckles went white against the table, watched her spine curve down low as she lowered her head. "Yes!" she hissed.

"Did you like it?"

"No. But he didn't want to do it," she whimpered. "I wanted to do it and he didn't and, when he finally did, it *hurt*."

Smoothing his hand over the silken skin of her butt, he leaned down and whispered, "When I fuck you in the ass, you'll like it...and it will hurt. Hurt so damned sweet, you will *beg* for more."

He pulled his hand away, dropping to his knees behind her. "Put one knee on the table. I want to see that little pink pussy open wider," he ordered.

As she lifted her leg, he watched the pink folds open, saw the glistening of her cream, felt hunger rip through him. He pressed his mouth against her, and groaned as the first hot, spicy taste of her exploded on his tongue. With a rabid growl, he feasted, spearing his tongue into her pussy, eating at her as she moaned and cried, climaxing against his mouth.

Her knee buckled, her position shifted and he caught her as he rose, easing her down until her upper body again rested on the table. As she gasped for breath, he bent over her and whispered, "You taste good." Then he straightened, pulling a condom from his pocket before he unbuckled his belt, easing the zipper down and shoving his trousers past his hips. He tore the packet open, rolled the latex down his length, keeping his eyes on the open petals of her sex. "Is this what you've dreamed about?" he rasped.

"Yes," she sobbed, her hands clutching at the table.

"Tell me about your dreams," he ordered as he finished fitting the tight latex over his cock, leaning against her and rocking his dick against the crease of her ass.

"Why?" she said on a moan. "You seem to know them all anyway."

"Tell me," he cajoled. "You want to be fucked?"

"Yes."

"Taken?" he teased, working one hand under her to pinch her clit.

"Yes. Hard, fast..." In a rush, she said, "I dream about being held down, tied up, fucked so hard it hurts and when I say no more—I want you to make me take more. I want to beg, and want to be teased—" she moaned as he dipped his fingers into the drenching depths of her pussy.

"Go on," he whispered, pumping his fingers in and out, his eyes narrowing to slits as he tried to imagine that tight little glove closing around his dick.

"I want to feel your cock in my ass. I want you to push me to my knees and make me go down on you, fucking my mouth until you come. I want to be spanked—I want to feel like I've never felt before," she gasped, pumping her hips against his hand, then thrusting her ass back so that he felt the silken skin of her butt against him.

"Hmmm... Good. Now beg me," he purred into her ear, rocking against her ass so that his length was cuddled between the taut, quivering cheeks of her ass. "Beg me..."

Vikky couldn't believe what she was doing. Blindfolded, spread out on the table, listening to somebody whose name she didn't even know, letting him spank her, letting him fuck her. The flesh of her ass stung—a hot, sweet little pain that made her ache for more.

And what she'd told him! Damn it, most of those fantasies were things she had never told anybody. And now she had told somebody she didn't even know.

The words he had just whispered echoed through her mind. *Beg me...* She shouldn't. *What woman in her right mind begged a guy to fuck her, just because he wanted to hear her beg?*

This one did. Because, damn it, this was *exactly* what she had been fantasizing about all her life.

"Please, please, please fuck me," she whispered.

"Whatever you want, baby," he crooned and the deep, slow cadence of his voice rolled over her skin like raw silk.

One big hand pressed low on her spine, the heat of it scorching her as he moved closer against her. Vikky trembled as she felt the broad head of his cock push into her, slowly breaching the quivering flesh of her sheath.

His hands shifted to her hips, holding her still as he forged just a little deeper, withdrawing, pushing back in just a little farther. He kept up that slow teasing rhythm and Vikky cried out each time he started it all over again.

Damn it, her pussy was throbbing, aching to be filled, and his slow possession was driving her crazy. His hands gripped her hips, bracing her against the table as she whimpered and tried to push back. He was so hot, so hard, stretching her flesh as he pushed inside.

"Be still."

She jumped, hot little arrows of lust dancing through her veins as he smacked her ass again. It tightened in her belly like a fist as he said, "Did you want to be taken? Or do you want to take? I think you said you wanted to be taken."

The words echoed through her head as she stilled under his hands, every hot, wild dream she'd ever had of a man taking her rushing to her mind. His hand returned to her hip and she held her breath in anticipation. He worked his cock into her slowly and she whimpered and cried, "Damn it, *hurry*."

"Hmmm, no way. This is the softest, wettest pussy I've ever had wrapped around my dick and I'm going to enjoy it completely. I'm going to fuck you so slowly that you beg me to let you come and I'm going to listen to you scream, listen to you moan and savor the feel of it as you come around me."

Well, he may have intended that. But she was too turned on, the pleasure was too intense, too close to everything she had ever dreamed — already she teetered on the edge of climax.

She cried out as he slapped her ass, her pussy convulsing around his cock. The orgasm took her by surprise, striking her in the belly with the force of a sucker punch, robbing her of air, making her see stars in the blackness behind her blindfold. A dam seemed to break inside her and she felt lost in the riptide as she screamed and bucked against him. The orgasm tore through her with breath-stealing power.

Over her head, she heard him swear and he burrowed in, holding steady and still, his cock pulsing inside the snug

Every Last Fantasy

confines of her pussy as she screamed and gasped her way to completion.

"Bad girl," he murmured as she came floating back to herself, feeling the tingling in her body, the stretched tissues of her pussy, the soft, furry lining of the blindfold against her skin.

Vikky whimpered as he pulled out. His voice a low, rough rasp, he said, "You almost had me coming before I was ready. So now, what are we going to do about that?"

The table felt cool under her cheek and she sighed, letting the coolness seep into her body as she listened to him. With a replete, sated smile, she said, "You never told me I couldn't come. You said you'd make me beg and scream and moan and you did."

He laughed as he turned her over. Her sweaty flesh clung to the table as she shifted onto her back, her hands automatically going to the covering at her eyes. "Don't touch it, babe," he murmured. "I guess you've got a point—I never told you not to come, did I?"

A sharp cry left her lips as his hand landed sharply on the pad of her pussy. Fire streaked through her even as her mind reeled from the shock of it. He had spanked her pussy. *Holy shit...* Shock, indignation and arousal warred inside her but, before she could figure out which one to give voice to, he slapped her again, and again.

"You can come, Vikky," he said quietly, his voice throbbing with intensity. "You know you want to—I can smell how hot this makes you. You like this... You've *always* liked this..."

Confusion whirled in her brain... Another slap, then he dipped two fingers inside, pumping his hand for three short thrusts, before withdrawing and slapping her again, his fingers now wet with the cream of her arousal.

Always? Nobody had ever spanked her pussy before but why on earth did those words seem *right*? Her body loved it, wanted more, craved more.

Why did it seem like he had done this before, spanking and slapping her pussy until she came?

He seemed determined to slap her into orgasm — alternately finger-fucking and slapping her clit. He started to follow each slap with a slow, thorough stroking of her clit, dipping his fingers inside her, pumping them, then withdrawing to spank the mound of her pussy.

Vikky whimpered, lifting her hips, hungry to feel him inside her again even as she creamed under every light paddling of his hand. The slaps became softer, lighter, teasing until she was ready to scream, to beg, to offer anything if he'd just make her come.

The orgasm was building, hot and powerful, making her skin feel too tight to contain her body. Inside her chest, her heart slammed against her ribs with erratic, hard throbs and air sobbed in and out of her lungs as she shrieked, "Damn you, make me come."

"That's all I wanted to hear," he whispered as his hand fell away. She barely had time to take a breath before he spread her thighs, draped them over his elbows and slammed into her, one deep, driving thrust that buried his length inside her to the balls, his heavy sac slapping against the seam of her ass.

She tried to scream but there was no air left in her lungs. Black dots danced in front of her eyes as he pulled out slowly, letting her suck in much-needed air. He thrust back inside her, hard and fast, then another slow withdrawal. He kept up that pattern until she was screaming with every breath she managed to draw.

"Hottest little fuck I've ever had," he whispered, levering over her body, moving higher and higher, so he could move against her clit as he fucked her.

She wasn't even aware of it as she started to plead, "I have to come—let me come, let me come…"

"Come for me," he crooned against her ear.

Déjà vu swarmed through her as she climaxed and screamed, clutching his shoulders while, behind the mask, she saw the face of the man from her dreams. But then his image blurred and just the echo of another man's face was there, but quickly gone, before she could tell who…

* * * * *

Hot, blatant satisfaction curled through him as she begged him to let her come, without him even having to prompt her. When she came around him, her pussy vised down on his cock so tightly that he could barely work it back inside of her and he started to come, exploding inside the latex barrier with a vicious shout.

He lowered his head to rest between the plump little curves of her breasts, dragging air into his lungs. Her skin roughened as goose bumps broke out over her body. With a supreme effort, he straightened, his cock leaving her pussy with a wet little pop.

So fucking tight…

With a groan, he swept her into his arms. "Bedroom, sugar," he said, his voice thick, his head hazy. Damn, he felt drugged.

When was the last time he'd had a woman like this? Elaina's face, the woman from his dreams, danced in his head and he groaned as he tried to clear her image from his mind. She wasn't real.

Vikky was real, very real.

So responsive, so hungry. She cuddled into his arms with a soft little sigh. He rested his cheek against her hair, drawing the scent of her sweet flesh into his system with a satisfied little groan.

Within five minutes, he was curled around her in the bed, gently tugging the blindfold from her face, but keeping her from turning to look at him. "Not today," he whispered. "Not today."

Every Last Fantasy

Chapter Five

She woke alone.

Jerking up in the bed, Vikky glanced around, searching for him, but she knew that she was wasting her time.

She was alone in the house.

For a long moment, she wondered if she had been dreaming but the little aches in her body assured her it had really happened.

The muscles in her thighs throbbed and the flesh of her pussy felt sensitive and swollen. Even her breasts felt a little sore.

Oh yeah, it had really happened.

And then there was the note taped to her window.

If you want more than one night, be waiting in your car tonight, downtown, in front of your work. Midnight. Wear just that cloak you like to wear around town.

No signature.

She snorted. No way was she wearing a wool cape without anything on under it.

She had one made of velvet that would work much better.

Erik wondered if he was risking blowing it by going to the bank at lunchtime. Vikky saw him and waved, a friendly little smile on her face. Just friendly...no knowledge. Nothing.

As he sauntered up to her window, he flashed a grin. "Wondering if I could talk you into lunch again," he said, forcing his voice to be easy, casual. "I had a lot of fun talking with you last week."

The smile on her face faded and she shifted, licking her lips. "Lunch?" she repeated.

He nodded, not sure whether or not to be put off by the sudden change in her demeanor. "Yes. And maybe a date? Later this week?"

"A date?" she said, her voice hitching, wobbling.

"Yeah, a date. You know, when a guy likes a lady and wants to spend more time with her? It's a social ritual that is pretty common in this part of the world," he teased.

She swallowed. He could see her throat move as she did. There was a faint gleam of regret in her eyes as she leaned forward, pitching her voice low. "Well, I've kind of met somebody."

"We had lunch just a few days ago," he reminded her. "Met him that fast? Got that serious?"

She flushed. "I don't know. I met him a few nights ago and..."

Erik could have crowed from the sheer exhilaration that tore through him but he couldn't even let loose the maniacal grin inside him. Keeping his voice level, he nodded, reaching out to flick a stray curl out of her eyes. "Okay, babe. Hope it works out."

As he turned around, walking away, he let the wide grin loose and he said a quick, urgent little prayer. Hell, yes, he hoped it worked out. He was losing his head over her. And quickly.

Vikky watched Erik walk away with some regret. She'd really had a nice time with him last week. But this other guy — damn it, who in the hell was he? Maybe she would find out tonight.

She sighed, brushing her hair back and pasting a bright smile on her face as Zeke Monroe stepped up to her window.

With five Mason jars full of coins.

Every Last Fantasy

Oh, wonderful.

There was something unbelievably erotic about walking out to her car, sliding into it, knowing that if anybody looked close enough, they might see the pale line of her naked body in the gap between the sides of the cloak.

The cold air snaked under it, teasing her legs, tightening her flesh. Her nipples hardened until they ached to be touched. And her pussy…oh, she was wet, slippery wet. She could feel it as she shifted on the seat, driving down the road, hoping she wasn't going to regret this naughty streak that was suddenly not just a little wide…but a mile wide.

It would get her in trouble some day.

A smirk crossed her face as she glanced at the speedometer and saw she was driving fifteen miles over the speed limit. Might even get into trouble *tonight*, if she wasn't careful.

Man, would she have explaining to do if she got pulled over wearing this. The cloak kept her decently, and legally, covered, as long as she kept her arms at her sides.

Hard to do, though, when she was driving. Once she got to the square, she closed the cloak over her lap and kept her hands tucked between her knees as she glanced around.

Nobody there.

So she waited. Ten minutes passed and she was getting irritated and cold. When she heard the knock at the passenger side door, Vikky jumped, stifling the squeal in her throat.

Slowly, she lowered the window, just a little.

And his voice drifted in to caress her ears. "So, you ready to try something else?"

"Ummm, depends on what it is," she said nervously.

He laughed, a low rough chuckle that had her belly jumping with something other than nerves. Well, it was a nervous sort of tension, she supposed. "Don't worry, sugar, nothing that will hurt you, I promise. I'd tear apart anybody who hurt you..."

Just those words and she felt wanted, safe, desired...all at once. And even the part of her head that whispered, *You are too trusting*, fell silent. For now.

Slowly, anticipation buzzing through her, she unlocked the door. "Can I get out?" she asked, forcing the question past her tight throat.

"Yes. We're going for a walk." She felt him come up behind her and shivered as his hands lifted to rest on her shoulders. "This isn't the cloak I told you to wear."

Softly, she said, "Wool and nothing else is pretty uncomfortable." His heat seemed to reach out through the warmth of her cloak, seeping into her skin, and the scent of his body swam in her head.

He chuckled. "I guess maybe you have a point there. So I'll let it go. I'd hate to have anything besides my mouth turning your nipples red."

She gasped, feeling said nipples tighten, the silk velvet of her cloak abrading them ever so sweetly.

"I want you to close your eyes. Can you keep your eyes closed and trust me to make sure you don't fall while we walk?" he said softly.

Without even thinking about, her lids dropped and she held out a hand, waiting. He moved around her and bent down, brushed his mouth against hers, and she greedily opened her lips, seeking more of his taste. He stood still, letting her explore and she moved forward, arched up against his chest and traced the shape of his mouth with her tongue. She pushed her tongue inside, caught his between her teeth and sucked it hungrily.

With a gentle laugh, he lifted his head, paused to nip gently on her lip and lick the tiny wound before he pulled completely away. "I think I like you," he murmured, walking around her and wrapping his arms around her body. "You aren't going to ask me permission over every little thing but you aren't afraid when I take charge, either, are you? So many women are afraid..."

She was. No doubt. But her hunger won out over that fear every damn time. "I'm not afraid," she said, even though her voice wobbled and she knew he had to sense her nerves. "But I'm not going to call you Master, either."

He laughed, a deep, slow rumble. One hand slid up, cupping her breast. She had a moment to wonder if people could see but realized that, even if they were standing in the middle of a puddle of light cast by the old-fashioned lantern-styled light posts, it was the middle of the night in Corydon. Who would even be around to see?

"I don't want to be your Master. Just your lover. As long as it's my way."

Well, she decided, since his way suited her to a tee, she had no problem with it. As his hand folded over hers, she allowed him to guide her down the walk. "Where are we going?" she asked quietly.

She felt his eyes on hers and flashed him a cheeky grin. "Just for a walk, sugar. Just for a walk."

She could smell the heavy scent of pine, and saw the faint glow of rainbow lights behind the thin shield of her eyelids. She suspected they were at the gazebo in the town square. Shivering, Vikky had a brief second to wonder if this was a good idea before his hands came up to again rest on her shoulders. Then he was pushing her down. "I want to watch you suck my dick," he whispered, one hand fisting in her hair.

A moan rose in her throat and sheer need started to gnaw a hole in her belly at his words. The light pressure from his hand made her try to tug her head away, just so he'd tighten his hold.

He did, his hand clenching in her thick curls, using that hold to bring her face closer to him. She slid out her tongue, wetting her lips in anticipation as she listened to the rasp of his zipper. Vikky caught her lip between her teeth as he dragged it down. Then he gave her hair a tight pull, urging her face closer.

Hesitantly, she reached up, touching her fingers to his cock, feeling him jump under her touch. Closing her hand around him, she leaned forward and licked the head daintily. "I'm waiting, Vikky," he purred, arching his hips and pushing the head of his cock past her lips.

Her body shuddered as she opened her mouth wider, taking him inside, sucking lightly on the head. Again, she moaned, a slow throb moving through her pussy as she followed the rhythm he set, his hand in her hair keeping her head in motion. "That's it, suck it, sweetheart. That feels so good. You like that?"

Like it? she thought as a weak whimper escaped her. *Damn it, I love it.* She pulled back, circling her tongue over the crown before sliding back down on him, feeling the pulsing of the vein along the underside.

With her tongue, she stroked that vein as she slid her head down as far as she could go. He pushed farther and she gasped as she felt the head butt against the back of her throat. Both of his hands were buried in her hair now and she could only imagine how they must look, this man whose face she hadn't seen holding her head still as he started to pump his hips, pushing his cock in and out of her mouth as she knelt before him, wearing a black cloak that would shimmer in the faint light.

With a devious inner smile, she raked her teeth along his flesh, biting him lightly and shivering as he swore and started to thrust harder and harder. Semen leaked from the tip of his dick and she greedily swallowed it, sucking it down, sucking harder, seeking more.

He growled just before he pushed in one last time and held steady, flooding her mouth and throat with hot, thick jets of seed. She swallowed it down as his hands fell away, letting her pull back.

Every Last Fantasy

Keeping her eyes closed, she tipped her head back and smiled up at him, tasting him as she ran her tongue over her swollen lips.

"Bad little girl," he whispered. And then he jerked her up, whispering harshly, "Don't you dare open your eyes." Before she could so much as gasp for air, he spread the edges of her cloak, spinning them around as he lifted her. Suddenly there was something hard and unyielding at her back as he braced her upright, wedging his hips between her legs and driving deep inside her—forcing his length completely inside her pussy.

She whimpered, throwing her head back and sobbing as he pushed ever deeper, feeling so much bigger, harder than he had last night. He rasped one thumb over her clit, lifting her higher, bracing her weight with his arm under her ass. Her fragile control slipped and she flew apart, climaxing in his arms with a broken cry, yet he kept surging into her pussy, the head of his cock rubbing over the tiny little notch buried deep inside her vagina.

She couldn't breathe. The force of another climax was on her—like ocean waves during a storm—slamming at her, knocking her down before she even recovered from the last one.

Harder and harder, over and over, he fucked her, from one climax into another, and another. Even in the cold air, sweat formed, leaving icy streaks of sensation on her body as it cooled in the frigid night. Her nipples ached, stabbing into the cold, hard throbbing little points that he, from time to time, pinched or licked.

It was too damn much. She couldn't breathe.

"Stop," she moaned. "Too much…please."

"Take it," he growled. "You said you wanted to be fucked, and fucked, and if you begged for me to stop, you didn't want me to. I'm fucking you, taking you, and I'm not stopping until I am damned good and ready."

She screamed as he shifted his grip and rode her harder, his pelvis dragging against her clit with every deep, hard stroke. "That's it," he said, his voice raspy, guttural. "Come again...scream more. Mine—you're mine. Mine to fuck, to spank, to keep."

One hand slid down to her ass and she quivered as she felt him stroking lower and lower...then she felt his fingers, wet with her cream, probing at the entrance to her ass. The new sensation slammed against her already sensitized body. "Going to fuck this ass," he muttered as he pushed slowly inside, the tight anal muscles resisting, causing a burning little pain to streak through her. "Push down," he whispered into her hair. "You're going to feel cock in your ass, just like you wanted, but you're going to be ready for it. So ready for it, you'll beg me to fill this tight little hole with every last inch of my dick."

Helpless, unable to resist, she whimpered, tears leaking out of her eyes as she pushed down. With slow, thorough intent, he completely penetrated, pushing deep inside the hot glove of her ass with his finger. The burning pain turned into fiery hunger as she shoved back against his hand, seeking more.

"I think I'll tie you up before I fuck this hot little ass," he purred. "Would you like that?"

"Yes," she moaned, and then she came again as he twisted his wrist, rotating his finger inside her.

He pounded into her harder and harder as she climaxed, the muscles in her pussy clutching at his cock. Against her chest, she felt his groan as he started to come.

The hot splashes of his come hit deep inside her—*inside* her. No condom. And she didn't care as she pumped against him, clutching at his hips with her knees and working herself up and down as he fucked his dick in and out...before finally, the choke hold of need released her and she could breathe again.

Erik stalked into the house and hurled his jacket away with barely restrained fury.

This little idea had backfired on him.

He was going to die inside if he had to let her go. He had to keep her. And not just for a little while, like before. *Can't lose her again...* Then he stopped, a scowl on his face as he murmured the words that had just echoed inside his mind.

"Can't lose her again...but she's never been mine to keep," he whispered. "At least, not until now."

His head was swimming, full of the unreal pleasure he had just experienced, and surging with emotions and thoughts he couldn't completely decipher.

She was driving him crazy. That was all. That taunting little brat of a woman was everything he had ever wanted and those hungers that raced inside of her were so in tune with his.

He wasn't promiscuous but he had fucked enough women to know that very few could possibly mesh with what he needed. And what he needed was a woman he could control...to some extent. But he also wanted one who was independent enough to want to take that control back from time to time.

Sex with her would never be boring.

Sex? No, that didn't describe the hungry, fevered episode in the town square's gazebo. That was more. Even more than lovemaking. That had to do with the heart, the soul.

Mating... A merging of her soul with his.

At least he hoped her heart and soul were involved. Because he was going to be damned disappointed — heartbroken even — if, after she had her fantasy, she tired of him.

Chapter Six

Vikky stumbled into the house with tears running down her cheeks.

She was going insane.

That had been the most erotic, most unbelievable experience of her life.

She had never felt anything like it before.

Except...*she had.*

She had done just that before, but on a night when it was cold and rainy and there was firelight flickering in old-fashioned street lamps around her. She could all but taste the rain on her skin, feel it beading on her flesh as strong hands flicked open the catch at her throat, making her cloak spill to the ground.

She had worn silk gloves, the kind you wore with a formal. And old-fashioned garters. Nothing else.

A man whose face she couldn't make out had urged her to her knees and she had taken the heavy width of his cock into her mouth, sucking on him until he had come with a rough moan.

He had turned her onto her hands and knees then, and driven his cock inside her from behind, his heavy weight crushing her to the ground as he had wrapped his arms around her. Pinning her flat between his body and the ground, his hips had pistoned back and forth and his cock had driven so hard and deep inside of her that she couldn't breathe.

After they had finished and calmed down, sweat chilling on her flesh, he had rolled onto his back, shifting her until she was cuddled against his side and she had looked up into dark green eyes that smiled down at her tenderly. "I love you, Elaina," somebody had whispered.

And she heard her voice say back, "I love you, too, Jacob. So much."

* * * * *

She called in sick.

She was losing her mind, so that counted as sick, right?

Not that she could go to the doctor about it. *Ummm...excuse me Dr. Neville, but I think I know what my problem is. I'm reliving a past life and I can't separate my lover from that life with the one I have now.* Yeah, that would go over real well.

She paced the house. In a fit of desperation, she packed up the things her aunt had left her, the mirror, the combs, all of it, as though it was somehow tied to these crazy memories. But then, before she had even gotten the stuff halfway to the attic, she was whimpering and crying, tearing open the box she had stored her mirror in and fishing it out.

Once her hand closed over it, she clutched it to her chest and gasped for air.

What's going on?

She started to put the packing material back in the box but something maroon caught her eye. She thought she'd emptied the box completely, but apparently not. Digging it out from the bottom of the box, she brushed away bits and pieces of material from the cover, staring at the old album with bemusement.

She opened it, and gasped when a letter fell out.

It was addressed to her, in her wacky, beloved old aunt's handwriting.

Darling Victoria,

I hope you enjoy the treasures I've sent you. Many of these things have been yours for longer than you've been alive. I haven't the words to tell you this in any way that would make sense, because until you remember, it would seem foolishness anyway.

There are answers within this journal. Be careful, for they are complicated and difficult. And do not look until you are ready to know these answers. Now, I know this all sounds terribly vague and bizarre. I am quite sorry for it but your mother refused to let me tell this while she was alive. She didn't believe it, you see. Although I knew who you were the minute I saw you the first time, she didn't believe me – perhaps she couldn't. So many people only believe what they can see with their own eyes.

After she died, you were so fragile, I hadn't the heart to put this on you and then I came to understand that perhaps your mama was right, even if it was for the wrong reasons.

She didn't ever want me to tell you – didn't think you needed to know. I believed you did but that, when the time came and you were ready to remember, you would. Something tells me that, as you read this, you'll find you are ready.

And you will remember.

All my love,

Auntie Gloria

Vikky licked her lips, absently stroking the album, as she read and re-read the letter.

Ready to remember? Remember what?

She could almost hear the echo of her aunt's voice as the words, *Remember...her,* floated through her mind.

Her. Elaina.

She had never heard the woman's name in her dreams until the flashback from the previous night. And it was a flashback, not a dream, not a figment of her imagination. It had happened. A long time ago, but it had happened.

Carefully, she opened the album, eyeing what looked to be an article from a newspaper, but it was yellowed with time and it read like no newspaper article she had ever seen before.

The album was full of them—a wedding announcement about an Elaina Montgomery marrying a Richard Whitehouse.

Every Last Fantasy

Then an obituary, it seemed. Richard Whitehouse, dead at the age of thirty-three from a wound that had been inflicted during a hunting accident.

Invitations that were handwritten, yellowing, faded. Many parties at various places. But the name Mary Spencer leaped out at her. Familiar... It echoed through her mind and suddenly her body, her surroundings, the album, everything around her seemed to fade away and she found herself standing in a crowded room, surrounded by people who wore clothes from a century long past. Watching as one woman stood between two men, screaming behind the silk gag in her mouth, her eyes all but blind with ecstasy as they fucked her senseless.

Then she was turning away, embarrassed, aroused, frustrated. Walking down a hall, she saw a woman giving a man a blowjob while another spanked her ass with a long, slender leather crop. Then she was alone in a room, desperately tearing off her clothes—a voice behind her murmuring, *Allow me...*

She turned around, and found herself staring at a man. Jacob... No, his face shifted and became somebody else... *Erik?*

Erik...and she suddenly knew the voice that had been whispering to her the night before, who was behind those letters. It was Erik.

Time seemed to whirl past her, dancing, picnics in the country, long nights spent living out fantasies beyond her wildest dreams. Painful pleasure. Sweet, slow lovemaking. His hands in her hair as he fucked her mouth. Walking outside her house to go to a ball wearing nothing under her dress—simply because he had told her so.

Then it all slammed to a stop and she found herself back in her carriage once more. A loud noise—gunshot—then the door to the carriage flying open.

Vikky opened her mouth, the scream that had been trapped in her throat for more than a century tearing free.

67

Chapter Seven

She wasn't at the bank. Erik stormed out of the building with frustration in his eyes.

Frustration, and some bizarre sense of terror.

Odd thoughts darted through his mind. Elaina… He had gone looking for her—they were supposed to meet—and she wasn't there… Where did she go?

Erik raked a hand through his hair, fisting it and pulling until his scalp burned while he tried to work through the tumbled mass of confused, chaotic thoughts. He was looking for *Vikky*, not Elaina. He'd never known an Elaina. Never fallen in love with an Elaina.

Then he stopped fighting it.

Yes, he had. Maybe not in this life, but he had. Fallen hard and fast, so desperately in love with her that he couldn't think or breathe without feeling her. They were going to get married—privately, because neither of them relished being under the watchful eye of society.

But when he went to get her, she was gone.

Gone.

The loud blaring noise of a car horn jerked him from the near trance. He looked around, feeling oddly out of place around the cars, the bright lights… He could almost smell the rain, the smoke from fires used to warm houses, all but feel the heavier, finer clothes he had once worn.

Okay. He had loved a woman named Elaina, and lost her. Was he transferring his emotions from this lost love from another life over to Vikky? *No.* Even as he turned the thought over in his head, his heart whispered, *You love Vikky.*

Every Last Fantasy

He suspected that was true. And fear raged through him, remembering the dreams where Elaina's face had faded away, leaving the grisly image of a dead woman's face floating in the water, a skeleton's image coming back to haunt him.

Desperate to see Vikky, just to know she was safe, he jumped in his car, pushing the car as fast as he could go in the small town. He squealed to a stop in front of her house and jumped out, running up to pound his fist on her door. And wait.

Vikky heard the knocking. Distantly. She lay in bed, tears streaming down her face, her body shivering. She couldn't move. Fear had locked her body down. Horror and pain coursed through her, leaving her feeling hot and cold, sweaty and sick. Even as she heard a loud crash and the door burst open, she couldn't do anything but lie there.

Erik came to a halt inside the door, staring around him, his heart pounding in his chest.

It thudded damn near to a halt as he fell to his knees, spying a thick album on the floor. One yellowed sketch caught his eye. A woman's face. *Elaina.*

...gone to the continent with new husband, Baxter Lyles...

Those words leapt out at him. He saw a man's face as he closed his eyes. Arrogant, lantern-jawed, over-large, shrewd eyes as cold as ice. *Lyles... Baxter Lyles.*

She had left him. Elaina had left him. Then the sharp tearing pain after he had leapt at Lyles, hideous pain blooming in his chest, knocking his breath away. Blood pumping from him, and then darkness.

Nothing else. He couldn't remember anything else.

Just that she had left him—and *that* pain went even deeper than that final pain, the one that had felt *very, very* final indeed.

A soft sound in the hallway caught his attention. Lifting his head, he stared at her, his eyes grim, jaw clenched. "Elaina," he whispered.

Her chin lifted. "You're Exxiled," she said quietly. He could see the slight quiver of her lip, the echo of pain in her eyes.

"You left me," he rasped, rising, his head spinning as he seemed to fall back through time to that day, suffering that bitter anger, that heartbreak all over again.

Tears flooded her eyes. "No, I didn't." A hoarse sob tore from her throat and she pressed the back of her hand to her mouth, spinning away from him as shudders started to rack her body.

Blind to everything but the pain he felt, he crossed the hall with two long strides and gripped her shoulders, spinning her around, a hundred angry accusations blooming in his mind.

But as his hands touched the bare flesh of her shoulders under the thin straps of her camisole, shock slammed through him, wrapping a fist around his throat and cutting off his air as the memories tearing through her mind leapt into his.

"Did you really think I'd not know?"

"Know what, Baxter?"

"About him, about what a whore you are. Oh, I know. And I will not be the laughingstock when you return to town and announce your marriage. Throwing me over for that American – "

Hands, hard, cold and strong, closing around a slim, pale throat, her neat nails digging into them as she kicked and scrabbled for breath. The air inside her lungs turned into a fiery hot agony as she struggled to breathe, to fight, but her resistance grew weaker...and weaker...until she was no longer even able to move.

A hideous pain bloomed in her mind and then there was darkness. She hid there, feeling safer...but then it was cold. So cold and wet... Water? She tried to suck air into her lungs and choked. Struggling, she tried to move but her arms were tied, her clothes were so heavy. *Down, down, down,* Elaina went, trying to escape the watery death that lay before her. It was hopeless, she couldn't breathe, couldn't move.

And then she could...but, as she moved, her body stayed still, locked in the depths of the river, as she drifted up and up... And when she looked down, she was staring at the murky water of the Thames River.

Oh, God. The words echoed in Erik's brain but his throat was too tight for him to speak.

Oh, God. Scrunching his eyes closed, he prayed, shoving the thoughts out of his mind. *Didn't happen. It didn't happen. Couldn't have happened.*

But a soft sob echoed through the room and he opened his eyes, unable to close his ears against the pain and fear. Staring into her soft blue eyes, he rasped out, "Vikky... Baby, I'm so sorry."

* * * * *

Vikky's hand shook slightly as she stroked the mirror. "I don't remember everything," she said haltingly. Flicking a glance at him, she forced a shrug and said, "I don't really want to. Most of what I remember is about Jacob—well, you. But that last night, I remember more. Leaving the house, the carriage ride home, a gunshot. Then Baxter Lyles."

"Don't," Erik whispered, shaking his head. His hands rubbed her back in slow, soothing circles as he cuddled her on his lap. "Don't do this to yourself."

She shrugged slightly. "It happened a long time ago—literally," she said with a soft watery laugh. Vikky licked her lips, resting her cheek on his chest, listening to the steady beat of his heart. "I don't understand what's happened lately. Two weeks ago—less, really—my life was normal. And now I feel like everything I've known is just not what it used to be. I'm not who I used to be."

"Yes, you are," he whispered, squeezing her tightly to him. He touched his fingers lightly to the surface of the mirror. "I remember this. Bizarre, isn't it? You started having dreams when you got the mirror, didn't you? That's about when I started having them."

"Fate," she whispered.

Looking up at him, she murmured, "Take me to bed. Make love to me, Erik. I want to look up into your eyes and know you're with me, know I'm safe." She had no more than finished speaking when he stood, and carried her down the hall to her room.

Her feet never touched the floor as he laid her gently on the bed, his hands catching the loose straps of her camisole and gliding them down her arms, leaving her naked in the watery light that shone through the windows. As he undressed, his gaze roamed lingeringly, lovingly over her body.

"How did I live all this time without you?" he whispered as he lowered his mouth to buss her gently.

"Erik." Twining her fingers through his hair, she tried to capture his mouth, but he merely chuckled, moving his mouth down the curve of her jaw, to her neck, raking the skin lightly with his teeth before kissing a hot trail down to the aching tips of her breasts. First one, then the other, he suckled them gently, his fingers teasing the plump little curves, his tongue curling around one nipple and drawing it deep. She gasped as he slid his knee between her thighs, spreading them apart. He sat back on his heels, staring at her and Vikky flushed, feeling the rush of blood spread upward from her breasts. His eyes darkened as he brushed the back of his knuckles over the waxed mound of her pussy.

"Damn, that's pretty," he muttered thickly. That harsh, guttural sound sent butterflies winging through her belly. Erik shifted, sprawling between her thighs and blowing a hot puff on air on her naked flesh. "Look at how wet you are." She shivered as he stroked one finger down the middle, parting the plump folds of flesh, his finger gliding through the thick dew.

Her breath froze in her chest as he slid his finger into his mouth to lick it clean, staring up at her from under the veil of his lashes. "Sweet," he purred.

Head tossing, Vikky squirmed on the bed as he slowly lowered his mouth to her pussy, sliding his tongue out and doing one slow, lazy circle around the tight bud of her clit. A soft wail escaped her as she reached down, twining her fingers through his hair, arching up against his mouth. "Soft," he grunted, working two fingers inside her wet sheath. "I love your pussy," he whispered.

Hot little chills raced up and down her spine, tightening her flesh, her lungs constricted as she whimpered hoarsely under his hands and mouth. Arching up, she tugged his hair and said, "Please!"

"I will, don't worry," he teased her as he continued to lightly pet her flesh, nuzzle her clit, all soft, feathery caresses that did everything to whet her appetite, and nothing to satisfy it.

Vikky hooked one leg over his shoulders, sinking her teeth into her lip. His teeth scraped over her clit, one rough touch, and she exploded, screaming as the hard little climax slammed into her belly. He groaned, pressing his mouth against her, one hand clutching her thigh, as he fucked his tongue in and out of her pussy with fast, shallow strokes.

As the tension left her, she was finally able to breathe and she sucked cool air into her lungs, staring blindly up at the ceiling as her heart slammed against her rib cage. His face appeared in her vision, stark and hungry. Slowly, lethargically, she lifted her arms and cupped his face in her hands, rising up to kiss his mouth. She tasted herself there and, under that, was the hot, spicy tang of man.

His hands cupped her hips and he pulled back, staring down at her as he pulled her toward him, draping her knees over his thighs. She stared at Erik, entranced, as he wrapped his hand around the base of his dick, holding it steady as he started to slowly push his way into her, the thick pillar of flesh stretching the wet tissues of her pussy.

Soft, shuddering cries sounded in the room. His harsh breathing echoed in her ears as he forged ever deeper, slowly, so slowly that she could feel the harsh jerking of his cock and count her heartbeats. She wrapped her hands around his wrists, pleading with him to hurry, to fill her, to fuck her. Love her.

"Always," he whispered, levering himself over her body, keeping her thighs spread wide as he wedged his hips between them, changing position in one fluid motion. Then he laced his fingers with hers, lowering his mouth to hers—driving the rest of his cock inside the wet well of her pussy with one long, hard stroke that stole her breath.

Her hands clutched at his, her nipples stabbed into the hot, hard wall of his chest. His face filled her vision and she could see nothing, smell nothing, sense nothing but him as he pulled out and surged back in.

"Love you," he muttered against her mouth, plunging his tongue deep. His big body tensed as she clenched the walls of her pussy around his cock and felt him tremble.

As his mouth pulled away long moments later, her head fell back and she gasped out, "I love you, too, Erik."

Those words were like a match to dynamite—explosive. He shouted out her name as he reared back and plunged deep, fucking her fast and rough, his cock pulsating and hard as she came around him.

The sounds of sex filled the air, flesh slapping against flesh, harsh breathing, a soft female cry. As he came, she threw back her head and screamed, her eyes vague and glassy, her nails biting into the flesh of his hands as she squeezed.

He flooded the hot depths of her pussy with his seed, groaning out her name as the chokehold of lust finally eased its grip on him and he could breathe, think, move. Just barely. He shifted to his side, cuddling her against him, kissing her brow as she shivered and clung to him, her breathing just as harsh and raspy as his own. His eyes closed, and memory flooded him.

Storming to her house, banging on the door...nobody there...door open. He stepped inside, staring around him, looking for some sign of her.

Then he saw Lyles. Standing at the top of the stairs, a dark, deadly smirk on his aristocratic face.

"Where is Elaina?"

Lyles laughed, the sound harsh and empty, sending chills down Jacob's spine.

"Out of your reach forever," Lyles said.

Dread flooded him. The metallic taste of fear, hot and potent, filled his mouth and he tore up the steps, shoving past Lyles to stride down the hall to Elaina's chamber. "Elaina!" he called out, voice rough and urgent.

The odd clicking sound behind him made him stop. Slowly, he turned and stared at Lyles, his eyes narrowing on the gun the other man held. "Oh, do not worry. You'll be joining her soon enough," Lyles said with a chuckle.

And then he pulled the trigger. Hot, burning pain exploded in his chest—the force of the bullet sent him spinning and he fell to the floor, trying to breathe, but unable to. His eyes opened slowly and he stared at the portrait hanging in the hall. Elaina...her face...fading, but he took the sight of her face with him into the darkness.

His eyes opened and Erik found himself staring at the ceiling, the memory clear and vivid in his mind.

A soft sigh sounded beside him and he reached out blindly, catching Vikky's hand as she stroked his chest. She asked quietly, "What happened to you...after? Do you remember?"

Angling his head, he stared at her, forcing a tight smile. With a shake of his head, he lied softly, "Nothing. Not important. Nothing mattered after you— After Elaina." Then he rolled over, pinning her underneath him, his eyes on her lips. Lowering his head, he kissed her gently, his cock nudging her belly as need for her filled him anew.

"Nothing," he repeated. "Until I saw you again."

GUILTY NEEDS
ಐ

Trademarks Acknowledgement

The author acknowledges the trademarked status and trademark owners of the following wordmarks mentioned in this work of fiction:

Armor All: The Armor ALL/STP Products Company
Coke: The Coca-Cola Company
Jack Daniel's: Jack Daniel's Properties, Inc.
Knock Out Roses: CP (Delaware) Inc.
Lexus: Toyota Jidosha Kabushiki Kaisha DBA
Pledge: S. C. Johnson & Son, Inc.
Taco Bueno: Casa Bonita, Inc.

Chapter One

The wind cut across the graveyard, cold and bitter, sharp as a knife and unrelenting. The rain continued to fall, every bit as cold and unrelenting as the wind. The cemetery was empty now, save for a couple of miserable souls—the workers waiting to shovel the wet earth over the gleaming, shell-pink coffin and two mourners.

Alyssa Hutchins
Beloved Wife
Dear Friend

That was it. It didn't seem to do her justice, her life summed up in those three lines. How could thirty years on this earth be condensed down to three damn lines? Bridgette Lancaster—Bree—knew just how little justice those lines did Alyssa. She hadn't been a dear friend. She'd been *the* friend—the kind of friend everybody should have at least one of. Not just the kind of friend you'd call when you were bummed over a guy, or when you needed to go shoe shopping. Not even just the kind of friend you'd call if you needed to bury a body.

Oh, God…she flinched as her mind played back memories of days when she'd stormed into the room she'd shared with Alyssa throughout college. Her best friend would take one look, then with a conspiratorial smile, she'd ask, *Where do you want to hide the body?*

Not that Lyssa could ever hurt anybody. She just didn't have it in her.

Where do you want to hide the body?

The body. Shit —

She tore her mind away from those memories. Harmless little comments tossed out to make each other feel better after a bad day. Maybe some day, Bree could look back and smile again. But she didn't know.

Alyssa had been the kind of friend who knew your every little secret, even those Bree wished nobody knew — especially not Alyssa. And she'd loved Bree anyway.

God, Lys. How are we going to make it without you? Bree thought, swallowing the knot in her throat.

Then her gaze was drawn to Colby. Colby Hutchins, Alyssa's husband…and Bree's darkest secret. The one secret she'd hoped Alyssa would never discover…

~ ~ ~ ~ ~

"Hey."

Alyssa turned her head and saw Bree standing in the doorway. She smiled, and even as thin as she had become from the cancer, the smile lit her entire face and made her beautiful. "Hey, yourself."

Bree came into the room and settled her hip on the edge of the hospital bed. When the doctors told them there was nothing left to be done, both Colby and Alyssa had insisted she come home. For the past three weeks, Alyssa had lived in the home she and Colby had built from the ground up, just three years earlier. Their dream home — built when a combination of luck and hard work had paid off for Colby and he'd hit the writer's version of the lottery, an overnight bestseller followed with an offer for more books, the kind of offer that would make a lot of people weep.

The money made it possible for him to take care of his dying wife without relying on a hospital. Private round-the-clock nursing care kept her as comfortable as anybody could hope for and Colby himself took care of giving her baths, brushing her thinning hair and coaxing her to eat or drink as often as he could.

Thankless work, Bree guessed, but all it did was make her love him more. If he was bitter over the lot life had handed him, he never showed it. Married less than seven years, they'd been talking about having kids soon, then a routine exam revealed something none of them could have prepared for. Cervical cancer—the rapidly advancing kind. Too advanced for surgery and, they soon discovered, too advanced for medical treatment.

By the time the doctors caught the cancer, it was just too damn late.

"Where's Colby?" Bree asked, taking the tube of lotion from the bedside table and squeezing some into her palm to rub onto Alyssa's hands. Colby had done her nails again—Bree knew it was his handiwork because of the slightly uneven strokes near the cuticles. Practically since middle school, Alyssa had given herself manicures every week and painted her nails in some vivid shade of red or pink with a fru-fru name that made Bree snort.

Closing her eyes, Alyssa smiled and said, "I made him leave the house for a while."

Bree laughed. "And how did you do that?"

"I told him I wanted some ice cream from Schone's. It's summer."

"Lime sherbet," Bree murmured, smiling faintly. "I'm glad you've got something of an appetite today."

Alyssa grimaced. "I don't have an appetite. I'll eat a little, but I needed him to leave for a little while."

"Why? I know he's hovering but—"

"It's not that." She turned her head on the pillow, studying Bree with solemn eyes. "I just needed to talk to you. I want you to do me a favor."

Fingers slippery with lotion, Bree squeezed Alyssa's hand. Alyssa squeezed back, but the lack of strength there was heartbreaking. She'd gotten so weak. Forcing a smile, Bree said, "You know all you have to do is ask. We need to go bury a body?"

"Just mine."

Bree flinched. It was a standing joke between them, that they'd help bury the body if one of them ever needed that kind of help. But it wouldn't be too long before a body was buried — Alyssa's. Bree couldn't think about that right now. "Lys—"

"Don't, Bree. Don't look at me and smile. Don't look at me and lie, tell me that I'm going to be fine. You and me, we both know I'm not. Colby knows it too, but he dances around it. Nobody can say it." She closed her eyes, took a deep breath, and then looked back at Bree. Her body might be physically weak, but her determination shown in her eyes. That strength of spirit that had driven every choice in her life and it hadn't faded a bit. "I need to say it without somebody telling me some pretty lie. I need somebody else besides the damn doctor to admit it to my face. I'm dying, Bree. Say it."

Bree's throat closed up. Shaking her head, she whispered, "Lyssie…"

"Say it. Lying about it doesn't change it and it doesn't help me. I need you to say it."

"Why?" Bitter, Bree demanded, "Do you think I don't know that you— Do you think I don't know?"

"I know you know." Her voice softened and Alyssa shifted, easing her body over a little and then patting the bed beside her.

Careful, mindful of the tubes running this way and that, Bree lay down beside Alyssa and stared at her through a veil of tears. Alyssa needed to hear it—for some reason, she needed to hear it from Bree. *We'll help each other hide the body*, they'd said over the years and they'd meant it. If they'd hide a body together, then surely Bree could do this. She took a deep breath and it shuddered out of her. "You're dying." A hard sob almost choked her, but she battled it back down. Not now. She couldn't break now.

Later. At home. She'd break then. But not now.

"Thank you." Alyssa closed her eyes. "You don't know how aggravating it gets when people keep lying to me, 'Oh, you look wonderful. You're going to be fine'." She snorted. "I don't look wonderful and I'm not going to be fine...well, at least not here."

She opened her eyes and smiled at Bree. "I had a visitor this morning—Danny Gleason."

"Danny Gleason..." Bree ran the name through her mind and finally came up with a face just barely remembered. High school. Major punk, into drugs, into alcohol—then a DUI had put him in the hospital and he'd ended up getting his left leg amputated. Sometime during his recovery, he'd "found God". Shit. Narrowing her eyes, Bree shoved upright in the bed and demanded, "Was he out here bothering you?"

Alyssa laughed and patted Bree's hand. "Calm down, Bree. He came out here because I had Colby ask him to. I..." her voice trailed off and she shrugged. "I had some questions. He's the kind of man with the answers to those questions. I've been so scared, but I'm not so scared now."

"After talking with Danny one time?" Bree winced immediately and wished she could take the words back. Hell, what did it matter if Alyssa found some sort of comfort in the life-after-death speech? What did it matter if she believed some ancient fairy tale about everlasting life, forgiveness and salvation? If it gave her comfort, what did it matter?

Sighing, she shoved a hand through her short, spiked hair and said, "I'm sorry, Alyssa."

Alyssa shook her head. "There no reason to be sorry. And yeah, one talk. But sometimes, just one talk can make all the difference. I'm not scared now—and I'm not so angry either."

"You haven't been angry, but hell, don't you think you're entitled?"

"What good does it do me?" Alyssa countered. "And yes, I've been angry. I lay awake at night, cussing everything I can possibly think of. But it doesn't make it any better and it doesn't make it even easier. It doesn't change anything, Bree. I hate being angry, I hate wasting what little time I've got left that way."

That was so totally Alyssa. If it didn't change things, didn't improve things, she didn't want to waste her time with it. Bree, on the other hand, nursed her anger, nursed her grudges, didn't waste her time giving a smile to a stranger because she had too much on her mind.

In so many ways, Alyssa was the better person. It shouldn't be Alyssa lying in this bed, but Bree. *Stop feeling sorry for yourself. You're here for Alyssa right now, not a pity party.* She forced herself to smile and hope it didn't look as fake as it felt.

But one look at Alyssa assured Bree that smile definitely wasn't fooling her. "Maybe I should give Danny a call, see if it can make me not so damn angry."

"You like being angry," Alyssa reminded her. Then she shifted on the bed and reached for the little gadget hooked up to her pain medication. It was narcotics, the kind that would put a grown man to sleep. The dosage was patient-controlled and Alyssa pushed the button with a sigh. "I hate needing this stuff."

Her lids drooped low over her eyes and Bree waited, wondering if the medicine was going to knock Alyssa out, but it didn't. She suspected the pain was just getting too bad for medication to control. "Do you need me to get some ice? A blanket?"

"No. Just that favor."

Reaching for Alyssa's hand, she said, "Name it."

"It's about Colby."

Bree's heart skipped then started to beat faster, faster, until it all but choked her. She schooled her features, years of practice keeping her from reacting, other than her racing heart. "What about him? He'll be fine, Alyssa. I'll be here if he needs me, but he's going to be fine."

"Sooner or later, yeah. I know he will. And so will you. But that's not it." She wiggled around and said, "Help me sit up, will you? I'm so damn tired of lying down."

A few minutes later, several pillows plumped up behind her back and the head of the bed elevated, Alyssa sighed. "Oh, that's better. I might make Colby take me out to the garden later. I've missed working in it."

"I bet your flowers miss you working on them. Colby's doing what he can, but he doesn't have a green thumb. I offered to help but he said he'd rather do it."

A grin tugged Alyssa's lips. "For me." She sighed, gazing out the window at the riot of colors blooming. "Maybe later you can take care of it. I know he's not going to keep messing with it after."

"Consider it done."

Silence fell and Bree found herself uncomfortable with it, nervous. It was weird, feeling nervous like this with her best friend. They didn't constantly need the silence filled, but today, it felt different. Edgy. Heavy.

A minute later, though, Bree wished for the awkward silence again. Her heart slammed up into her throat, and no matter how hard she tried, she couldn't keep her reaction under control. Hell, she couldn't say anything.

Patiently, Alyssa repeated the question she'd asked only seconds earlier. "Do you love Colby?"

Some trite lie formed on the tip of her tongue. *Of course I love him — he's your husband and that makes him almost a brother to me.* But she couldn't. It was just too wrong — lying to her dying friend, claiming to feel a fraternal emotion toward a man who inspired anything but fraternal thoughts. In the end, all she could do was just sit there and blink away tears.

"What's going on, Lys?" she asked woodenly.

"I'm taking care of unfinished business—namely you and Colby. You do love him, don't you?"

Mute, Bree nodded. The knot in her throat was so damn huge, it felt as though she was going to choke on it.

It was words, she realized. Apologies that she should have given long ago. "I'm so sorry, Alyssa. I just...I can't...I...I..." Jerking her hands away, she covered her face and whispered, "I'm sorry."

"Why? I love him. I know how damn easy he is to love."

"He's your husband, damn it. I shouldn't..."

"You can't control who you love. It's not something we're given a choice in, Bree. And it's not something we *should* choose. Why be sorry for something you can't control? You've never done anything about it, you've hidden it, you've never let it come between us. It's not as if you ever tried to take him away from me."

Appalled, Bree stared at Alyssa. "Why would I? He loves you. He—"

The faint smile on Alyssa's mouth had Bree swallowing the rest of her words.

"I know." Shaking her head, Alyssa said, "There's nothing to be sorry for."

Although it wasn't a question, Bree couldn't help but respond to it anyway. "I never did anything, Lys. I swear, I never—"

"Bree. I know," Alyssa said softly. She held out her hand—thin, frail and trembling.

But when Bree linked their hands, she felt as though she was the weak one. Physically, emotionally and mentally. "You're not mad at me? Why aren't you mad at me?"

"No, I'm not mad. Hell, Bree, how could I be mad?"

"I don't get how you can't be mad." Sick inside, humiliated, scared, miserable, Bree tried to pull away. "I'm sorry." She couldn't think of anything else to say.

Alyssa, impatient as ever, rolled her eyes. "Enough with the 'I'm sorry' crap, Bree. It's okay. I'm not mad. Besides...it makes the favor a little easier."

"Favor." Wary, Bree pushed off the bed and backed away. Tucking her hands into her pockets, she asked, "I think you need to explain about this favor."

"I don't want Colby to be alone," Alyssa said quietly. Her voice was faint, a bare echo of the deep, throaty purr it had been since her mid-teens. But for all its softness, it was firm. And certain. Very, very certain. "He deserves a happy life, but I know him. He's going to lock himself away over this and brood. And brood. And brood and brood. You get the point."

"He's good at brooding. But he'll be okay."

"You don't seem to get what I'm wanting here."

Rolling her eyes, Bree said, "That's because you haven't asked me for anything. I'm not quite the mind-reader you are."

Alyssa smiled. "That's just because you like being the stubborn type. If you weren't so damn stubborn, you'd know what I was getting at. I want you...with Colby."

"With Colby." Bree blinked, the words rattling around in her mind, but not connecting, not making any sense. "What do you mean?

"I mean, I want you with Colby," Alyssa said.

Bree's jaw dropped. Alyssa grinned.

"What in the hell are you talking about?"

"I want him happy. I don't want him hooking up with some money grubber and I don't want him spending his life alone."

"Alyssa, he's thirty years old. He's got..." her voice trailed off. Man, it just seemed so damn wrong to talk about this right now. With Alyssa dying and her husband out chasing after lime sherbet for her.

"I know he's young. I know he's got time. But life's precious. It wasn't until this happened that I realized just how precious it is. I don't want him to waste a minute of it. Colby, he's every bit as stubborn as you are. Remember how long it took him to ask me out?"

"Nearly a year." They said it together. Colby was the classic sexy geek come to life. A computer whiz, a science-fiction buff, a state chess champion and he was also an all-star athlete. Between his SATs and his ability on the basketball court and track, he'd gotten a full scholarship.

The three of them had grown up together and sometime during their freshman year, the two girls had both noticed how cute the brainy geek from eighth grade had gotten. It was Alyssa, though, who went after him. And Alyssa he fell in love with. She'd chased after him most their freshman year and just after tenth grade started, he finally asked her out. They'd been together ever since and Bree had spent most of that time in quiet envy. It might have been enough to break the friendship of some girls, but although Bree had privately fallen more and more in love with Colby, Alyssa was the sister she'd never had and she wasn't about to lose that.

"Alyssa, you know I'd do anything for you, but you're asking me for something that's not in my control. What do you want me to do, show up here and tell him you want me to be with him so he doesn't grow old alone? So he isn't lonely or spending hours on end brooding? I can't control that. Besides, why in the hell would he want me? He has to want me, or it doesn't matter..." she trailed off, licked her lips and reminded herself that Alyssa already knew. It wasn't such a secret anymore. "It doesn't matter that I love him, unless he wants that from me."

"And I think he will. You asked why in the hell he would want you, but I've got a better question. Why wouldn't he?" Her lids drooped and her voice started to slur from exhaustion.

"You need to get some rest, Alyssa."

"I've got plenty of time for that. Not so much for this." She started to shiver, though. Bree grabbed the blanket and tucked it around Alyssa's thin body. "I know I can't control him. But I also know him. He's going to hide—either in his work or in anything else that distracts him. Don't let him hide, and when the time is right, I want you to do the same damn thing I did. Go after him."

"You'd think, after twenty-five years, you couldn't surprise me, Lys." Shaking her head, Bree started to pace the room, staying close by the bed and keeping an eye on her friend. But she just couldn't stand still. Not right now. "But I don't get it. I can't understand this."

"There's nothing complicated about it. I want the two of you happy. You're my best friend, he's my husband—I've never loved anybody the way I love you two. Why wouldn't I want you to be happy?"

"I couldn't do this—if we were switched, I know I couldn't do this."

Alyssa smiled. "Baby, I think you probably could...but I'm glad it's me. And not you."

Snarling, Bree demanded, "How in the hell can you say that? It damn well should be me. It's not like I've got a man who's going to grieve if I die. The only important person I'd leave behind is you. Damn it, it *should* be me!"

"No. If it should be you, it would be— Bree, I'm glad it's not." She closed her eyes and a heavy, sighing breath escaped her. "I'm not as strong as you are, Bree. I'd break. If I had to watch this happen to you, watch this happen to anybody I love, I'd break. I'd do exactly what most of my other friends have done and just disappear. I couldn't handle it. But you can. You're strong, Bree. You always have been."

You're wrong, Bree wanted to say.

But Alyssa was already asleep.

Blinded by tears, half-sick with guilt and disgust and despair, Bree headed for the door. She had to get out of here. Get on her bike, crank it up and let the wind blow it all away. If she went fast enough, far enough, maybe she could escape it.

You're strong, Bree. You always have been. Shit, what a pathetic joke.

She plowed straight into a rock-hard chest. Jerking away, she mumbled, "Sorry," and tried to go around Colby but he caught her arm. Heat flared along her skin where he touched her. As guilty as she felt, she loved the feel of his body touching hers, even a touch as innocent as this.

"Bree, are you okay?" His tawny eyes left her face, looking toward the room he shared with Alyssa. "Is Lys…?"

Forcing a smile, she said, "She's asleep. I'm just… I just need to breathe."

His fingers fell away from her arm, but before she could escape, he rested his hand on her shoulder. Through her T-shirt, she could feel the heat of him, the strength. His thumb swept along her skin, leaving goose bumps in their wake and Bree flushed painfully red. Tucking her chin against her chest, she held still, tried not to breathe, not to move.

"It's hard."

Startled, Bree looked up at him. He had that lopsided smile that Bree had so fallen in love with, but it was sad. "Watching her day after day, seeing how much she hurts and how tired she is. Some of our friends, well…they can't take it. They've pretty much stopped coming over. Some of them don't even call any more. You don't know how much it means to us that you keep coming over every day."

Shit, could she possibly feel any guiltier? Didn't seem possible, but Bree realized she was wrong. As he innocently stroked her shoulder and tried to make her feel better while his dying wife lay sleeping, Bree stood there, her body reacting to his touch as though he had stripped her naked and put his mouth on her. Her guilt grew until it encompassed everything.

Haltingly, she said, "She's my best friend, Colby. I need to be with her."

"I know. And she needs you."

Tears blurred her eyes. Rage churned inside, trapped, unable to find any outlet. She started to shake and she knew, just knew she was going to break. Alyssa was wrong. Bree wasn't strong—she was about as weak as they come.

Colby sighed.

So attuned to him, Bree heard the soft catch in the sound and unwittingly, she lifted her head and looked at him. Saw a muscle jerk in his jaw, saw the suspicious glitter in his eyes. But then he blinked and it was gone. "I'm glad she has you with her, Colby."

Then she rose on her toes and kissed his cheek. If she breathed in the scent of his skin a little deeper than she should, it wasn't intentional. If she shivered a little and wished she had the right to kiss him differently, it wasn't because she could help it. She loved him—she always had.

But no matter what Alyssa had asked of her, this wasn't something she could do.

The next day, Alyssa was gone. Colby had lain down with her for a nap and she died quietly in his arms while her private-duty nurse was at lunch. Bree was five miles away, bringing Alyssa some cinnamon candy from a small, family owned candy shop, even though she knew Alyssa wouldn't eat them. She'd spent the past day trying to come up with the words for Alyssa, words to explain that what Alyssa wanted wasn't something that Bree could really do.

But it was too late for explanations.

Too late to tell her best friend how sorry she was, even if Alyssa didn't want apologies.

Too late to do anything but watch as Colby quietly and emotionlessly went about the task of calling the doctor and everybody else. Even though the nurse told them she'd handle it, Colby did it all. And when it was done, when all the final arrangements were made, he walked out of the house without looking back. She didn't see him for two days, not until the visitation, and he didn't say a word, didn't speak to anybody. It was almost like looking at a robot...

~ ~ ~ ~ ~

Today was no better.

He continued to stare down into the gaping hole in the earth. The silent agony on his face had her eyes tearing up. She wanted to say something, wanted to do something, but what was there to say? What was there for her to do?

Still, she couldn't just stand there. Making her way across the sodden earth, the heels of her boots sinking into the soggy ground, rain pelting her face and hair, she went to stand with him. "Colby."

At first, he didn't even act as if he'd heard her. Then, slowly, he lifted his gaze from Alyssa's coffin and stared at Bree as though he'd never seen her before. She gave him a half-hearted smile and held out a hand. "Come on. You don't need to keep standing in this rain."

Off to the side, a sleek, dark-gray limo waited, but if she knew Colby, there was no way he was going to climb into it. He'd followed the unspoken funeral protocol, done what was expected, arriving at the funeral home and sitting in the front pew as Danny spoke about Alyssa's too-short life and the grace she'd shown even when death came for her. The words had been like ashes to Bree and she had no doubt the words of comfort and commiseration had been every bit as bitter for Colby.

Now the funeral was over and there was nobody but them. He'd likely throw protocol to the wayside.

As though following her line of thought, he glanced toward the limo and his lip curled. "Do me a favor?"

"Anything."

Jerking his head toward the limo, he said, "Tell them to get the hell out of here."

Guilty Needs

She rephrased a little, explaining to the driver that she'd get Colby home. As the limo drove off down the narrow black road, she made her way back to Colby. Inside her boots, her feet were damp and cold. Her sodden skirt didn't do anything to block the chilly wind.

Keeping her arms wrapped around her midsection, she joined him once more at the graveside. "Let me drive you home, Colby."

He shook his head. His dark hair was plastered to his head, he was soaked through and through, but he showed no intention of getting out of the rain. "I can't go back to that house right now, Bree. I can't do it."

She suppressed a sigh. Pushing her dripping hair back from her face, she hooked her arm through his and tugged. To her surprise, he fell in beside her. Every step away from Alyssa's grave was painful and by the time they reached her car, tears mingled with the rain on her face. "We'll go to my house for a while, if you want."

"Fine." His voice was hollow. Expressionless. His eyes were every bit as empty. "Whatever."

Help him through this…she knew that was what she needed to do.

But Bree had no idea how. How did you help a person who had lost the other half of their soul?

* * * * *

It still didn't seem real.

Colby had known this day was coming for weeks now. He had feared it for months, ever since Alyssa's lab tests came back showing positive for cancer cells. But still, it *did not* seem real.

It might if he let himself think about it, but he wasn't ready to do that.

Fortunately, Bree seemed content to drive in silence, not trying to force him to talk about anything, anybody. Since they'd climbed into the big black truck she drove when she was working, she hadn't said anything.

It was meticulous inside the cab. Bree owned her own landscaping service and usually her truck was a mess of notes, gloves, fast-food boxes, clipboards on the inside and the truck bed was full of tools and equipment.

But today it was pristine. Closing his eyes, he leaned his head back against the headrest and breathed in the scent of Armor All, rain—and Bree. The woman always smelled like flowers. Incongruous as hell, such a soft, feminine scent on Bree, a woman who stood five-foot ten, hauled around forty-pound bags of soil and regularly kicked ass on the basketball court. With the rain pounding down around them and the quiet in the truck's cab, he almost—almost—felt comforted.

Almost felt as through he was ready to think about it.

A knot formed in his throat and he realized he wanted to talk—needed to talk. But then the truck stopped and the engine cut off. Opening his eyes, he saw that they were in Bree's driveway. The thirty minute drive had passed far too quickly and dread churned inside him. He didn't want to go in there.

What the hell had he been thinking?

Bree's house would be almost as bad as home—pictures of the two women all over the place, ranging from when they'd been cute kindergarteners showing off gap-toothed grins up to the barbecue at the house last summer. Up until Alyssa had gotten too weak to leave the house, she'd still come over to Bree's house two or three times a week and many of those times, Colby had been with her. This place had practically been a second home.

But Bree was already climbing out of the truck. She stood in the driveway, and once more, rain soaked her through. She stared at him levelly and he knew she wasn't going to go inside until he did. Some lingering courtesy had him climbing out of the truck, and as one, they headed into the garage. The garage was half office space, half storage space and unlike her truck, it was always meticulously organized.

Inside the house, warmth wrapped around him and he abruptly realized how damn wet he was. He stripped out of his overcoat and Bree took it from him before he could figure out where to put it. As she moved away, he pushed a hand through his wet hair and glanced down and realized he was dripping all over the floor. He took off his shoes — they were probably ruined after standing in mud and rain all day. Something knotted in his chest as he carefully put them on the floor by the door. Alyssa had made him buy the damn things a few years ago, telling him he needed to own something besides three or four pairs of tennis shoes, a pair of hiking boots and a very badly abused pair of loafers.

Dragging his eyes away from the shoes, he headed into the kitchen and found Bree standing at the counter, making up a pot of coffee. The strong scent of it already filled the air. Grabbing a couple of paper towels, he mopped the rain from his face and hands. His clothes were still damp but at least he wasn't dripping now that he'd taken off the shoes and coat.

"You want something to eat?" Bree asked quietly.

"No."

She grimaced. "Me neither. Okay, lets try this — have you eaten anything today?"

Colby blinked and tried to remember. No. He was pretty sure he hadn't. Yesterday at the visitation, one of their friends had tried to talk him into a sandwich, but after two bites, he'd put it down. As far as he could recall, that was the last thing he'd eaten and he wasn't entirely sure he'd eaten much of anything since…

Since…

Shit. The burn of tears stung his eyes and he turned away from Bree and rubbed a hand across his face. He wasn't ready to do this. Not yet. Not here. Where and when escaped him, because Colby wasn't too certain he'd ever be ready to acknowledge reality, but he sure as hell didn't want to do it here and now.

"Colby."

He glanced at Bree over his shoulder and gave a half-hearted shrug. "No. I'm not really hungry—" he tried to tell her but she was already rooting through the refrigerator.

Over her shoulder, she said, "I'm not hungry either, but we both should probably eat. I bet I haven't had a regular meal this week." Turning to face him, her arms full of lettuce, lunch meat and tomatoes, she cocked a brow at him. "Have you?"

"No." Colby couldn't remember the last time he'd been hungry, though. Probably a couple of months, ever since the visit to the oncologist had revealed that the chemo hadn't worked. The thought of eating anything held about as much appeal as going back out into that cold, driving rain.

Heaving out a tired sigh, he dropped down onto one of the stools at the breakfast bar. "What is it about funerals and food? Megan Lowell kept asking me about a wake, asking if she should bring something."

Bree slid him a glance. "Yeah. She cornered me and told me that the two of us, me and her, should take care it, have it over at your place. I told her you probably weren't too keen on that idea."

"Good." Something occurred to him as she pulled a knife from a chopping block and started to slice a tomato. "You ran interference for me the past couple of days. Thank you."

She shrugged. "That's what friends do. You've got enough to deal with right now."

Shaking his head, Colby said, "I'm not dealing with anything that you're not dealing with. Alyssa—" his voice cracked and it took two tries before he could finally speak without worrying he'd break before he finished the sentence. "You two were like sisters. This is every bit as hard for you as it is for me. But you..." his words trailed off and he had absolutely no idea what he was trying to say. "Just—well, thank you."

Lame as hell.

Thank you? That was the best he could say to the woman who'd all but put her life on hold to spend time with Alyssa before she died? The best he could say to the woman who had been like a sister to his wife?

She gave him a sad smile. "You don't need to thank me, Colby." For a moment, tears glittered in her dark-gray eyes but then she looked away. When she looked back, her gaze was clear and level. "I haven't done anything I didn't want to do."

"Yeah." He ran a hand over his wet hair and then reached for his coffee. "I know."

They both fell silent, mostly picking at the sandwiches Bree made, but Colby made himself eat half of his, hoping maybe Bree would do the same. Her cheeks had a faintly hollow look and there were shadows under her eyes. He guessed she hadn't been eating or sleeping any better than he had. Outside, the rain continued, a heavy downpour that showed no signs of letting up.

When Bree rose from her seat, he followed, pausing to refill his coffee cup. Bree made it the same way he preferred it—black and strong enough to send caffeine zipping through the system on one sip. The caffeine barely penetrated the fog in his brain today, but it was warm.

Right now, he desperately needed the warmth. He felt frozen through and through, yet it wasn't because of the rain or his wet clothes. It could be ninety degrees in Bree's house and he'd still feel chilled to the bone. He found Bree in the small den tucked just off the kitchen, kneeling in stocking feet in front of the fireplace. She slid him a look over her shoulder and said, "I don't care if it is May. I'm freezing."

"Yeah. I know the feeling." He would have offered to do it for her, but before he had even set his cup down, she had the beginnings of a blaze going. In moments, flames were dancing over the logs.

Bree settled down in front of the fireplace, drawing her knees to her chest, automatically smoothing a hand over the long skirt, adjusting it so that it draped over her legs. Colby sat down in the fat wing chair off to the side and stared at the flames, letting himself get lost in them. It was easy just then not to think, to sit in front of a warm fire and pretend he hadn't just lost the most important person in his life.

He never realized he'd fallen asleep until the phone jerked him awake. He jumped, for a moment not recognizing where he was and his mind automatically went to Alyssa — he needed to check on her…but then he remembered.

In the distance, he could hear Bree's low, quiet murmur and he blocked the sound of it out, tried to still the storm churning inside him. He needed to get out of here. The rain was still coming down, although from the sound of it, the downpour had lessened a little. He came up out of the chair, wadding up the blanket Bree must have draped over him. He threw it on the footstool and headed out of the den, hoping he could grab his jacket and slip outside.

Remembering that his car was still at the funeral home, he paused, but then just shook his head. He didn't give a damn if he had to walk. He didn't really have a destination in mind anyway — just not home. That was the only thing that mattered. He didn't know if that house could ever be home again. He'd built it for Alyssa.

It hit him then, just as he went to grab his coat from the hook hanging by Bree's side door. It hit him like a ton of bricks dropping down to crush him. Slamming a hand against the wall, he tried to keep from buckling under the weight. What hit him weren't tears — such a simple term couldn't explain the pain that boiled up from deep inside and threatened to kill him as it clawed its way out of him.

He never heard Bree come in, just knew that suddenly she was there, slipping an arm around his waist, then the other, holding him as he finally let himself acknowledge reality.

Alyssa was gone.

There would be no one last chance to hope and pray for a miracle, no more nights where he could lie awake and watch her while she slept. Gone.

*****

Her back was on fire and her left leg was so numb, she was pretty sure it would take an hour just to be able to get any feeling back in it—if she was ever able to move. But she didn't care, didn't say anything. They were half-laying, half-kneeling, with his head in her lap and the fingers of one hand twined with hers, holding on as though he'd never let go.

Her own tears were blinding her, but she blinked them back.

She wasn't sure when the silence between them started to change. It wasn't a comfortable silence, or an easy one, but the grief between them kept it from being awkward. But it changed—more on her part than his—or at least she thought it had. But then she realized that his free hand rested on her thigh and his thumb was stroking back and forth. Through her skirt, she could feel his warmth and every slow stroke was enough to make her heart skip a beat. He wasn't even aware he was doing it, she suspected—any more than she was aware that she was lazily stroking a hand through his silky hair.

The tension spiked between them and slowly, Colby lifted his head. His pupils were dilated with just a thin sliver of amber showing. The hand on her thigh stilled—tightened. His gaze dropped to her mouth. She hated how easily her body reacted, hated that she wanted more than anything to close the distance between them and press her lips to his. Hated it. Just as she hated knowing that she was weak enough to give him anything he might need, even if it was just some sort of comfort sex.

She hoped that wouldn't happen, yet somewhere inside, part of her hoped it would. Colby might need comfort, but she needed him. She'd always needed him and she'd never had the chance.

His lashes drooped low, shielding his gaze. A harsh sigh shuddered out of him and then he shoved to his feet. Without looking at her, he walked out of the kitchen, pausing only long enough to grab a key ring from the small bowl by her phone. She heard the engine of her bike revving out in the driveway. As he pulled away, she thunked her head back against the cabinet at her back and closed her eyes.

"Nice work, Bree."

* * * * *

Two days later, she found the keys to her bike in the mailbox, along with a scrawled note from Colby. She read the familiar handwriting and felt her heart twist in her chest, felt the sting of tears in her eyes.

Taking a trip. Need to get away.
C.

Yeah. She definitely understood that—she'd give just about anything to get away from things for a while, away from a house where there were a hundred memories of Alyssa, away from a life that held a thousand reminders of just how lonely Bree's life had become.

But she wasn't going anywhere. She had a business to run and it was one she'd been neglecting far too much since Alyssa had gotten so sick. She headed into the house, but instead of grabbing a bite to eat and a shower, she just tossed the keys onto the counter and headed back outside. If Colby was gone, now was as good a time as any to make good on at least one promise to Alyssa.

The big one, she still wasn't sure she could keep, but this one was easy.

Chapter Two
A Year Later

Even in dreams, she haunted him.

Hell, *worse* in his dreams.

When he was awake, Colby usually managed to jerk himself back in line if his wayward thoughts drifted toward her a little too often—something that happened more than he liked, but he could control it.

When he had a hard time doing so, he could use the emotional version of taking a cold shower—he could think of his wife. That did it every damn time.

But when he was asleep, those rules didn't apply.

In his sleep, he wanted to think about her, fantasize, dream...

Touch.

Taste.

Fuck...love.

Caught in the dream, he tossed on the bed, his hands clutching at tangled sheets as he lay alone.

In the dream, he wasn't alone.

She was with him—always with him...

~ ~ ~ ~ ~

"I need you..." she whispered as Colby turned to Bree and pulled her against him.

Her long, dangerously curved body pressed against his, her hands fisted in his hair as he lost himself in her. Covering her mouth with his, he nipped and sucked on that full lower lip until she opened for him.

Pushing inside, he drank her in, stole as much of her taste as he could while his hands got busy stripping the clothes from her body.

Simple, casual work clothes hid a body designed to tease a man to the breaking point. Under those clothes, those killer curves were almost bare, hardly covered by skimpy wisps of silk and lace. Silk cupped her breasts, lifting them high while a scrap of lace and silk stretched across her full hips and between her thighs.

Tearing his mouth from hers, he stared down at her body, at the way her breasts rose and fell with each ragged breath, the way the muscles in her belly contracted as he skimmed the backs of his fingers along the smooth, golden glow of her skin before dipping them inside the low-cut panties she wore.

She was wet.

Through the silk panties, he could see how wet she already was, and he wanted—needed—to lie between her thighs, pull that lace aside and taste her. Touch her.

Drive her so close to the edge that she screamed out his name. Drive her until she was as insane, as needy as he.

Working his way down her body, he stripped the panties off and pressed his mouth to her dripping core. She smelled sweet—too damn sweet, too damn good. The taste of her pussy was an addiction he couldn't handle, but he couldn't pull away either.

He licked her, sucked on her clit, fucked her with his fingers until she shoved up on her elbows and grabbed his wrist, working herself against his hand and sobbing out his name.

She came—and in that weird way of dreams, it shifted and reformed around him before he had even had time to savor her climax.

He could still taste her, still ached to feel her even as he stood on the floor in some darkened, unfamiliar room while Bree knelt before him. Her mouth—soft and sweet—wrapped around his dick while he fisted his hands in her hair and fucked her mouth. She hummed deep in her throat. He felt the vibration of it clear down to his balls.

Colby kneaded her scalp, groaning and rocking against her as she whimpered and clutched his hips—holding him tightly, holding him close, her nails digging into his flesh as though she feared he'd pull away.

Not that he would. Not that he could. For as long as this lasted, he was going to enjoy it—and damn it, he wasn't going to come in her mouth. He wanted to come inside her pussy— deep inside. So deep that she could feel him in the back of her throat.

The wall at her back seemed to appear out of nowhere as he pulled her to her feet and urged her backward, gathering all those ripe, lush curves.

"Wrap your legs around me," he muttered against her mouth, almost reluctant to speak for fear of shattering the dream.

Oh, he knew he was dreaming.

His dreams were the only place he could let himself think about Bree without guilt. Dreams couldn't be controlled, they could only be dealt with and he figured dreaming about fucking her was a sight better than hunting her down to do it.

In real life, he could, and would, control himself.

But in his dreams…Another weird shift and they were no longer standing in an unfamiliar room, but lying on the bed, Colby sprawled between her thighs while he licked her, while he fucked her with his tongue until she wailed out his name and begged him to fuck her with his cock.

Begged—as though she were as desperate for him as he was for her.

"Please, Colby—damn it, I can't stand it."

Guilty Needs

He crawled up her body, cupped her face in his hands and kissed her, deep and hard. "You'll stand it. You'll take it. We need it...I need it," he growled against her mouth as he pushed her thighs wide and settled between, with his weight braced on his hands.

Tucking the broad head of his cock against the mouth of her pussy, he waited until she reached for him before he took her, before he fucked her.

Before he loved her.

Over and over, harder and harder, until she wailed out his name and raked her nails over his shoulders. When her cries faded away to soft, exhausted mewls of pleasure, he slowed...braced his weight above and stared down into her flushed face.

Waiting.

For her eyes to clear, for her breathing to calm, for her heartbeat to slow. Then, hooking his arms under hers, he cradled her head in his hands, tangling his fingers in the short, gleaming strands of her hair and tugged until she lifted her mouth to his.

Slowly, he kissed her.

And slowly, he started to move.

Deep. Hard. Slow. Even when she started to rock under him, lifting her hips to his and trying to force him deeper, take him faster, he held steady. He nibbled on her lower lip, kissed his way down sweat-slicked flesh and caught one nipple in his mouth, sucking and licking, then shifting his attention to the other breast.

The ache in his heart, in his balls expanded, spreading through his entire body, until the hunger and the need threatened to consume him. The need to come was a vicious, twisting pain, but he wouldn't do it.

Not yet.

He couldn't let this end...not yet.

Because once it ended, he'd wake up…and he'd be alone again…

~ ~ ~ ~ ~

Alone again.

Colby came awake with the sheets twisted around his legs, his hand wrapped around his dick, pumping furiously, the orgasm just two seconds away from blowing the head of his cock off.

Gritting his teeth, he arched his back, closed his eyes and tried to grab the dream, tried to lose himself in it as he stroked his cock to orgasm.

Couldn't think—not yet. Couldn't remember—not yet.

His heavy length jerked in his hand and he groaned as semen started to spurt from the tip, coating his hand and belly. Breathing raggedly, he stroked himself through it, until he'd emptied himself.

Then, with guilt gnawing at his gut and loneliness burning through his heart, he opened his eyes and stared sightlessly up at the ceiling.

* * * * *

The first thing Colby noticed was that the property had been tended to.

The second thing he noticed was that the mailbox wasn't full to overflowing—there wasn't even a copy of the Sunday paper from yesterday. Of course, he hadn't paid the bill in…twelve months. They'd probably stopped delivery months ago.

Shit, for all he knew, the house had been repossessed and sold, wasn't even his anymore. This was what happened when you just disappeared and left everything behind.

Shoving a hand through his hair, he drove up to the house and parked on the semi-circle in front. At the end of the arc, it curved off to the right, disappearing behind the house where there was a three-car garage and a pool that would most likely need a massive overhaul before it could be used. He climbed out, leaving his bag in the car for now. Weird, he'd expected the house to have that deserted, vacant feel to it but it didn't.

So what if the damn place got sold? he thought, unsure if he cared or not. Part of him didn't want to care—this house wasn't a home anymore.

But he also wasn't entirely sure he'd be happy if it had been repossessed. Not that he'd have a leg to stand on. It wasn't as if he'd been keeping up on the payments. He'd spent the past year roaming around the eastern half of the country, doing his damnedest to forget anything and everything about his life—at least for a while.

He'd come back to take care of this place, get it off his hands, so it was weird to discover that he *would* mind if the place had been sold.

He hadn't written a word, hadn't read a book, hadn't spoken with anybody he knew, just gone from town to town, working odd jobs here and there. He'd taken a sizable chunk out of his savings account just before he left and lived on that money until it was gone, then he'd gotten by on what he could make with the odd jobs. He'd made his way through the Carolinas, down the coast to Florida, up to Alabama, with no particular destination in mind.

The past few months, he'd worked in Mobile, doing construction for a while, then waited tables when the economic slump had hit the construction industry. The days had passed in a surreal blur.

Endless nights passed slowly, haunted by dreams that left him aching and sick with guilt. Quite a few of those nights, he ended up relying on strong, hard liquor to quiet the dreams.

He'd been functioning just fine, taking one day at a time, one drink at a time.

Then the dreams got stronger. The need for a woman's touch had threatened to drive him crazy. But he didn't just want *any* woman's touch. He wanted Bree's touch. Craved it. Needed it.

That need fueled the guilt that he lived with and one drink just wasn't enough at night. He started needing two. Three. But the more he drank, the worse things got...because he starting hearing voices.

No. Not voices. Voice. One voice. Alyssa's.

Brought on by guilt, grief and loneliness, no doubt. And the alcohol probably didn't help. Of course, when he hunted down every last drop of booze he had in his apartment and dumped it down the drain, the imaginary voice of his wife would go quiet.

Didn't happen.

Hoped that maybe the dreams would fade if he just worked himself into exhaustion.

That didn't happen either.

Still, he kept away from the alcohol, made himself get through each day as it came.

Refused to think about anything beyond what he had to do to get through the days and nights.

But a day came when he found himself looking at a calendar and it hit him.

A year.

His wife had been gone almost a year. He'd walked away from his life almost a year ago. Though he didn't much give a damn about his pathetic, empty life, it occurred to him that he did have some loose ends to wrap up. The house, for one.

Bree was another loose end, but not one he was all too anxious to deal with. All he needed to do was tell her goodbye, tell her thank you.

Guilty Needs

Hot, sweaty dreams aside, guilt aside, she'd been there for him, for Alyssa, and it would be nice if he could tell her thanks without falling apart in front of her.

But the house first. He'd face Bree in a day or two. Maybe. If he could get his head on straight.

If the place had been sold, he doubted he'd be able to get inside. But to his surprise, his key worked. He opened the door and the silence of the place hit him square in the chest.

Quiet. Way too quiet.

There'd always been music playing or the TV on. Alyssa talking on the phone with Bree— *Shit, don't go down that road.*

But it was too late. His eyes closed as he thought of her and a stab of guilt hit him anew. Even a year later, he could recall how he'd almost done the unforgiveable. How close he'd been to kissing her, how close he'd been to reaching out and grabbing whatever comfort she might have been willing to give him.

But it wasn't guilt alone. It came with desire and he swore, passed a hand over his eyes, and tried to pretend he wasn't having a flashback to puberty when his dick got hard out of the blue and stayed that way until he locked himself in the bathroom and jacked off.

This was worse than puberty though, and the damn dreams that haunted him at night didn't help. He needed to stop this, stop thinking about Bree like that, stop thinking about her...period. It was messed up.

Why?

The whisper slid past him, a kiss of air against his ear.

If he let himself think about it, he just might admit his wife was haunting him.

Too many dreams plagued him and very few of them made sense. Well, the ones where he got his hands on Bree— those made sense. The dreams where he stripped her long, sexy body naked, dreams where she wrapped those strong, sleek thighs around his hips and took him inside. Those made plenty of sense.

There was something exotic about Bree, but there always had been, even back in school. He hadn't ever told Alyssa, but there had been a couple of months in high school where quite a few of his wet dreams had been centered on her best friend.

Bree was built—1940s movie-starlet built—with round, ripe breasts, hips, a tight, sweetly curved ass and a mouth that always looked just a little bit swollen, as though some guy had just kissed her. The way Colby too often dreamed of doing. She had serious gray eyes that tilted up at the corners, glossy black hair—worn short and smooth—golden-brown skin, and long legs that would wrap around a man's waist and ride until he begged for mercy.

Back in high school, he had quietly enjoyed those dreams without ever acting on them. Then, much like now, he was pretty much an introvert and the thought of asking Bree out would have been enough to have him stammering and tripping over his tongue. So he had dreamed about her, watched her, blushed when she looked his way, and that had been it.

But then Alyssa had started flirting with *him*, teasing *him*, and he'd been lost. The dreams about Bree faded and he'd been just fine and perfectly content to have Alyssa start taking the starring role.

The problem was that the dreams had started coming back and only hours after he'd buried his wife.

That was one serious problem.

Why is it such a problem?

A cold chill rushed over him and goose bumps broke out on his arms. Going crazy. He much preferred to think he was going crazy than being haunted.

Over the past month, it had steadily gotten worse. At first it was just early in the morning or late at night when he was exhausted, but now it happened almost around the clock and it didn't matter if he was tired or not. He heard a voice and he didn't need some shrink to explain why the voice sounded an awful lot like Alyssa's. He missed her and he felt guilty because maybe he didn't miss her enough—after all, he wasn't dreaming about *her* at night.

Blocking the voice out, ignoring the questions, he moved through the quiet house. He frowned, finding the entire place spotless. There was no dust, no stacks of mail, nothing. He hit the kitchen for a glass of water and automatically, he stopped in front of the refrigerator and opened it. It wasn't exactly stocked. Most of what was in there were staples—a carton of eggs, soft drinks and bottled water, a half-empty gallon jug of water.

The sight of the jug had him frowning. It was the same kind of water that Bree took with her while she worked. He glanced out the window toward the gardens.

They were pristine. Perfect. They looked better now than they had the entire time he had lived here and that was what clued him in. One look at the blooming flowers and carefully cultivated shrubs and trees, and Colby knew why the house looked so damn good. Why there wasn't any dust, why the house was clean, the grass was cut and the mail wasn't piled up to the ceiling and back.

Bree had been taking care of everything.

Everything—well, maybe not everything. She couldn't be paying the bills. But he realized, less than ten minutes later, that she had been doing that too.

Not just taking care of the house, the mail, the gardens. She'd taken up accounting too. Skimming his accounts, he saw that regular mortgage and utility payments had all been set up to automatic payments and his royalty checks were being deposited into his account. Bree was the only person who could be doing it. He couldn't think of another soul who would take care of the landscaping, the house...and his bills. Not to mention that there were only two people who had a key to his house—Bree and Callie Watkins, the lady who came in a couple of times a month to clean. And he couldn't quite see Callie doing all of this.

Something heavy weighed on his chest. Shit. Yet another reason to talk with her. It was the last thing he wanted to do, but he couldn't avoid it.

He really didn't want to see her or talk to her.

Not all of it had to do with the fact that seeing her was going to rub salt into open wounds. He could deal with reminders of Alyssa. Hell, sometimes he went out of his way to find things that reminded him of his dead wife.

What he had a harder time dealing with were all the guilty needs that punched through him on the rare occasion that he let himself think about Bree.

With the anniversary of Alyssa's death coming up in less than a week, he definitely didn't need his mental mess about Bree raining down on him.

But apparently fate had other plans.

He heard the truck coming just a little while later as he sat in his office going through his accounts. The records were meticulous, notes made in a neat ledger about each deposit, listing the amount, the payer and the date deposited. The checks had been from his two publishers and the check stubs had been filed accordingly.

Also filed away were several letters, some that had come via postal mail, others that had come through email and all of them were from either his agent or his editors. The last one was dated six months ago. He wondered briefly if they'd given up on him and then he paused to wonder if he even cared. The answer to that was no. At least not now. He didn't have a story in his head and he had no desire to try forcing one.

He'd finished up the books he had left on his contract a while back. He'd been ready to start discussing a new contract right about the time Alyssa found out she had cancer and he'd hadn't been able to think about anything other than her at the time. At least he didn't have to worry about breach of contract.

Colby blew out a breath as the truck headed up the drive, pulling up behind his beat-up old car. He'd sold the Lexus a few months ago when money had been really tight. The clunker in front of the house definitely didn't seem to fit. Pushing back from the desk, he headed out of the office and saw Bree.

For one second, his heart all but stopped at the sight of her. Tall, her short hair tousled around her pretty face, her body clad in the simple, casual work uniform she wore—a green T-shirt and khaki shorts. Shit, the things that woman could do for clothes. Colby suspected she could wear sackcloth and ashes and he'd still feel his heart stutter in his chest at the sight of her.

Swallowing, he took a deep breath and hoped he could manage to speak around the knot in his throat. Moving closer, he watched her through the windows framing the front door.

Through the glass, he saw her reaction when she caught sight of him.

Her eyes widened and her mouth opened. She slicked her tongue across her lips as she slowed to a stop.

For a moment, neither of them moved and then he made himself take a step forward just as she did the same. She reached the door before he did, but instead of coming inside, she just waited. Frowning, Colby opened the door and stood to the side, studying her. "Since when don't you just walk in?"

She swallowed. He could see her throat work under the smooth gold of her skin and he had the urge to bend down and press his lips to that soft, smooth skin. Her shoulders moved in a restless shrug. "I dunno."

He gestured for her to come inside and finally, she did, but he got the impression she really didn't want to. "You've been taking care of things for me."

She glanced over her shoulder at him and shrugged. "Yeah."

"Thank you."

"You don't need to thank me."

He opened his mouth to say something—he didn't know what—but Bree took off down the hall, leaving him standing there with his jaw hanging open. He jerked it closed with a snap when he realized he was watching the slow, lazy sway of her hips as she headed away. She had a pair of work gloves tucked into her back pocket but nothing could detract from the absolute perfection of that ass.

"When did you get home?"

Forcing himself to uproot his feet, he followed her into the kitchen and watched as she poured herself a glass of water. "An hour ago."

She paused in the middle of raising the glass to her lips. "An hour ago..." she repeated.

Then she shrugged and took a sip. "If you had let me know you were coming home, I could have bought some groceries and stuff for you."

He shook his head and settled on one of the scoop chairs nestled up against the breakfast bar. "I can't really say I've come home. But it's time I figure out what I'm going to do."

"Did the lawyer finally catch up with you?"

Colby blinked. "Lawyer?"

"Fred Whathisname? Whoever was taking care of things for Alyssa. He keeps calling me and reminding me..." her voice trailed off.

"About the will?" Colby asked.

She nodded, focused intently on her glass. As though sensing his scrutiny, she looked up and lifted a shoulder in a half-hearted shrug. "I know he's got a job to do, but I really don't want to keep hearing about her will, ya know?"

"Yeah." Grimacing, Colby dragged a hand through his hair. The thick, black strands of it had gotten so long, they hung in his eyes. He desperately needed a haircut, but he just didn't care enough to mess with it. "Shit. You know, I never even thought about that. I just wanted to get things settled with the house."

He blew out a sigh and lifted his gaze, studied the kitchen. It was bright and cheerful, full of little touches that Alyssa claimed would make it a fun place to cook, though Colby had suspected she had more fun thinking about cooking than she would actually doing it. "I came back to sell the place. I just don't think I can live here."

She was quiet for a minute. She licked her lips and Colby found himself following the path she took, eying the plump, wet curve of her lip. When she finally spoke, he cursed silently and made himself focus on her words. "So where do you want to live?"

"I have absolutely no idea."

Finally, the somber look fell away from her lips and she drawled, "Well, it might be wise to think about that before you do much else."

Colby shrugged. "I dunno. I've been doing all sorts of things the past year without thinking them through in advance. It's actually not too bad."

She lifted her brows. "Colby being impulsive. Now that's a switch."

He had another impulsive urge just then, to go around the bar and corner her against the counter, press his lips to hers. See if that body of hers felt as good as it had in his dreams. See if she tasted half as sweet. Instead, he pushed away from the counter and went to get a bottle of water from the fridge. Taking his time to open it, he said, "I'm sorry I just disappeared like that. I'm sorry you felt like you had to step in, the way you did."

"Colby."

He didn't want to look at her.

Every time he did, those guilty needs of his reared their ugly heads and he wanted nothing more than to grab her and haul her close. *Then do it.* He hunched his shoulder defensively as the whisper sounded right in his ear. Turning away from it, he faced Bree and wondered if she'd heard.

No. The look on her face was one of calm patience, not confusion or fear.

Besides, he reminded himself, *why would she hear it?* The voice was just a guilt-induced hallucination. Just guilt—not actually the voice of his wife. No reason for anybody else to hear it.

"Colby, I did it because I wanted to, not because I felt like I had to."

Then she lowered her glass and slipped out the back door. Moving to stand at the door, he watched as she jogged down the steps and drew a pair of gloves from her back pocket. Colby stared at the perfect, round curve under the faded denim and swore. Thunking his head against the glass door, he muttered under his breath, "You're fucked up, Hutchins. Seriously."

* * * * *

Colby...

Shit, she couldn't believe he was here. That he was back. Her heart had yet to settle back to normal and it was a miracle she hadn't stuttered every time she had tried to speak to him.

Even now, she couldn't get herself under control.

Of course, it didn't help that she knew he was watching her. She could feel it, feel his eyes on her as she worked in the flowerbeds, pulling up stubborn weeds, thinning out the day lilies that were already blooming in a riot of yellows and pinks. She'd thought maybe she was just imagining the weight of his stare but as she finished up in one flower bed and moved to another, she saw him standing at the window.

Staring.

It was a weird look, intense, probing, as though he was trying to see clear through to her soul, but at the same time, it was almost like he didn't really see her. Bree started to wave to him but then he turned on his heel and moved away from the window.

Finally, she thought. Maybe now she could focus on the job at hand instead of thinking about him, worrying about him...dreaming about him. All of that could happen later, when she was home, safe and alone. Where she didn't have to worry somebody might look at her and see all the secrets she tried to keep hidden.

Bit by bit, she relaxed, losing herself in the pleasure of the job. Hers wasn't an easy job—it was hard, manual labor, very often of the back-breaking kind. But she loved it. Loved planting things and watching them grow.

Sweat trickled down her forehead as she finished the particular flowerbed she had been working on. Absently, she swiped the back of one gloved hand across her brow, inadvertently leaving a streak of dirt. She blew out a satisfied sigh and then looked back at the flower beds she had yet to do.

And found herself staring at Alyssa, or rather, through her.

After a year, she'd finally learned to stop jumping when she saw Alyssa's ghost. But today wasn't a normal day and she just barely muffled her yelp. "Damn it, Lys."

Alyssa smiled. "Girl, you look like you've seen a ghost."

"Ha, ha."

"Bree, you really do need to lighten up. Live a little." Her voice had a weird echo to it, rather like she was talking from the bottom of a well.

"So says the ghost," Bree muttered, shaking her head. Grabbing her work tools, she headed to the next flowerbed. Sinking to her knees, she started weeding with a vengeance and hoping that if she ignored her, Alyssa might go away.

But it hadn't ever worked before—wasn't going to start working now. Alyssa plopped down right in front of Bree, so suddenly that Bree ended up sticking a hand right through her as she grabbed a pair of pruning shears from the bucket she kept her tools in.

Hissing, she jerked her hand back and glared. "Don't you have some harp-song-on-a-cloud date to keep?"

Setting her jaw, she started pruning a Knock Out Rose bush. Alyssa snickered. "Harp song. How boring. You really think dying is about playing harps?"

"Oh, geez." Since Alyssa didn't seem interested in moving her transparent tail away from the rose bushes, Bree abandoned her pruning shears and moved on to thin out the pansies that were threatening to overtake one of the many small flowerbeds.

"He missed you."

The sad honesty in Alyssa's voice caused a knot to form in Bree's throat.

"I know you missed him."

"Him missing me doesn't account for much." Sighing, Bree tugged off her gloves and stared down at her hands. They weren't a lady's hands. Strong, capable, with palms calloused from her work and nails she kept cut brutally short. Her skin was a smooth shade of pale caramel, a gift from the mother she'd lost back when she was a baby. Her gray eyes came from her father—though she didn't know him either. He'd dumped her on his sister within a few months of having her dumped at his doorstep and he hadn't ever looked back.

But it was his eyes she saw staring back at her from the mirror. Her aunt Cara had eyes the same shade of dark gray. Cara hadn't been prepared to suddenly become mama to a two-year-old child but she'd done the best she could.

Bree didn't suffer serious self-esteem issues. She knew what she looked like. She was attractive and when she put half a mind to it, she might even be beautiful. She preferred jeans over just about anything else and kept her hair cut short just so she didn't have to spend as much time messing with it. Still, she was pretty.

But she wasn't Alyssa.

She wasn't the woman Colby had fallen in love with.

She was a friend. In his eyes, that was all she'd ever be. Delusional ghosts... Bree figured being grounded in reality wasn't much of a concern for them anymore. Quietly, she repeated, "It doesn't matter if he missed me. Yeah, I missed him too. But he missed a friend, Lys. That's all I ever was to him. That's all I'm ever going to be."

Alyssa rolled her eyes. "Man, you are so stubborn."

Bree blinked, then snickered. "Me? You're the one hanging around here, determined to play matchmaker. A year, Lys. It's been a year. And you're not showing any signs of moving on."

With a melodramatic sigh, Alyssa said, "I can't move on until I know you'll be happy. Both of you."

Tugging her gloves off, Bree shoved her damp hair back from her brow and then fisted her hands on her hips. "You can't force this to happen, girl. Things happen because they are meant to, not because you force them." Rising, she strode away, determined to get a little peace and quiet.

Of course, the way her luck ran, Alyssa would just follow her.

But to her surprise, that didn't happen.

She settled down in a flower bed near the back of the garden and worked in peace and quiet. It occurred to her that Alyssa had given up a little easier than normal this time, but maybe that was because Alyssa was finally getting the point.

Chapter Three

Alyssa didn't understand the deal with being dead but it wasn't what she'd expected. She hadn't gone on to some glorious place in the sky, she wasn't roasting in some pit of endless torment and she hadn't ceased to exist either.

She hadn't intentionally clung to the land of the living, but apparently, in her subconscious, that was what she was doing. She faded in and out of conscious existence, sometimes lost inside herself for hours, days at a time. But never for too long.

It had happened again, just now. One minute she'd been talking to Bree, teasing her, chiding her, nagging her and then, just like that, Alyssa was gone. Time passed and she wasn't even aware of it, just that Bree had left and now Alyssa was alone in the house with a man who refused to see her.

She wasn't always here—here being on Earth. Sometimes she was someplace…other. No place she could describe, but it seemed as if it were a prelude to what waited, if she could just move on.

She wasn't always alone there, either.

People came and went. Some lingered for just a few heartbeats, but she'd been told that others had waited there endlessly. Trapped—trapped by their memories and regrets from a life that was over.

She didn't want that. She didn't want to be trapped between life and death, here and now and the hereafter. Which mean she had to move past what held her bound to her life. According to what she had been told, at least. And she believed it. It made sense.

Colby and Bree—they were the only people who mattered to her any more. None of the others from her life even seemed real. Just them. Almost surreally real, if that made sense. Thinking of one of them was all it took to go to them. She'd been watching them almost from the moment she breathed her last.

Bree had seen her the very first night but Colby continued to fight the knowledge. If he didn't want to see her, she couldn't force it on him. It had frustrated her to no end, but now she was glad of it. Maybe his stubborn refusal to see her could come in handy.

A wistful sort of yearning moved through her as she found herself in their bathroom, staring at him through a steamy panel of glass. He was in the shower, blissfully unaware of her. Leaving her to stand there and stare at him and remember. Lost in the memories, she thought of the way his hands had felt on her, the way he had touched her—careful, gentle—as though he feared he'd bruise her or mark her somehow.

She didn't miss sex. That was seriously weird, but she attributed it to being dead. Sex was for the living. She did miss the idea of it, missed being close to him, able to touch him. But it was a distant ache, almost as though he'd been lost to her for years and years.

The pain wasn't fresh, it wasn't vivid and it hadn't been, not even from the first. More weirdness to death, she supposed.

And another weirdness—her ability to know what they were thinking.

It was as though the words passing through their minds created a sound only she could hear. Now that had taken a while to get used to. Hearing his grief had been harder on her than anything else since her death. Sometimes it was still so raw, if she could have wept with him, she would have.

But his pain had lessened over the past few months and Alyssa knew if he'd just give himself a chance, he could let her go. Whether Bree believed it or not, Colby was ready to move on and Alyssa was damn well going to do whatever she could to convince him to move on to Bree.

Leaning against the marbled countertop, she watched as Colby finished his shower. When the door opened, she studied him. A frown darkened her face and the downward spiral of her thoughts made the room's temperature drop a few degrees. Angry or upset ghosts had a chilling effect but it wasn't until she saw him rub his arms that she realized what she was doing. Reining her thoughts in, she tried not to think about how lean he'd become. He'd lost too much weight over the past year.

Shoving away from the counter, she moved toward Colby, testing him. He never once glanced her way. She wondered once more why he could hear her but not see her. Bree was the rational, grounded type. Colby believed in ghosts, spooks and Big Foot. He should be the one seeing her, not the other way around.

Alyssa waved a hand in front of him, but still, he didn't react. Satisfied, she said, "She loves you."

He stilled.

How her voice sounded to him, she really didn't know. For all she knew, she sounded like herself, just more distant. That was what Bree said—as if she spoke from the bottom of a deep well.

She trailed a hand down his arm, her fingers lingering to touch the gold band on his third finger. "It's time to take this off, Colby."

He jerked away, his hand clenched into a protective fist. His gaze came up, searching the room, but he wasn't going to see her. So Alyssa settled for resting a hand on his chest and stroking downward. Down. Down. He felt abnormally hot to her, but everything seemed warmer than she remembered.

Why should he be any different? He had secured a towel around his waist but she slid her fingers inside it and tugged. He hissed, eyes going wide as he backed away.

"You don't want to spend the rest of your life alone," she whispered, remaining still as he grabbed his jeans from the floor and pulled them on over his wet, nude body.

"I'm going insane." He scrubbed a hand down his face. "I am going fucking insane."

Alyssa laughed. "You're not going crazy."

A muscle jerked in his jaw as he finished buttoning his jeans, but he didn't say anything, just stared off into the distance. She started toward him. "She's been waiting a long time for you."

This time, his gaze flew toward her, tracking the sound of her voice. But he still didn't see her. "Why did you come home, Colby? It wasn't about this place. It doesn't mean anything to you. Not anymore."

One thing Colby was certain about, if he was going crazy, he was pretty sure it was natural for some part of his brain to still argue that he was sane and rational. Even if the voice sounded like the echo of his dead wife. So the soft, almost amused assurance, *You're not going crazy*, didn't do a damn thing to reassure him.

Crazy people didn't really think they were crazy, he figured.

And crazy people definitely heard voices.

Did they feel people touching them, even when they were alone in a room?

Shoving a hand through damp, tousled hair, he tossed his towel in the general direction of the shower and said aloud, "I'm leaving now."

A low, sad laugh filled the room.

He turned to go, determined to just ignore his current hallucination. It would go away, sooner or later, right?

"Going to keep hiding away, Colby? How did that ever solve anything?"

He stopped in the doorway. Slowly, he turned around, but there was nobody in there. He saw nothing. His voice hard and firm, he said, "I am not hiding."

Then he left the room.

Something light, oddly soothing, touched his shoulder. He hissed and jerked, scanning the room. "If you're not hiding, then go find her. She's the reason you came back. Not this house. Admit it. Even if you can only admit it to yourself for now…stop hiding."

He wasn't going to hide. He didn't come here to hide.

He came to tie up loose ends and decide what in the hell he was going to do with his life. That had nothing to do with hiding.

As he made the thirty minute drive to the cemetery, he even managed to almost make himself believe that.

Then he saw Bree sitting by the grave as he made his way up the path.

She's the reason you came back…

He hadn't seen her since she'd left his place a week earlier and he really didn't want to see her now.

Liar! Okay, well at least that thought actually felt like his own and it wasn't ringing in his ears like the echo of Alyssa's voice.

Stop hiding.

He wasn't hiding. He just…well, he wasn't so sure he wanted to see her yet. That was all. But the memory of that soft chastising kept him from backing away, even though he wanted to.

It would have been easy enough to leave. She hadn't seen him yet and since he hadn't seen her bike or her truck in the main parking lot, he figured she'd parked in one of the smaller ones. He could just avoid her until she left, make this first visit to his wife's grave in privacy.

He didn't though.

That voice kept whispering through his mind and he had to wonder if maybe his hallucinations weren't on to something.

She's the reason you came back...

The house didn't matter to him.

Hell, his career didn't matter to him. It had been a year since he'd written a damn thing and he couldn't care less. Even though he knew he should.

But the house, his writing, his career, none of it seemed real. Nothing seemed real anymore, not since Alyssa had died in his arms. Well, nothing except dreams that made him hot with lust and sick with guilt. Until Bree had walked back into his life seven days earlier, or rather, until he had walked back into hers, nothing but those dreams had affected him.

Seeing her made him feel more alive than he had felt since losing his wife and if not for the guilt choking him, he might have even enjoyed it. But the guilt, man, it was killing him. How wrong of him was it to think about how damn pretty she was as he joined her at his wife's grave? He laid a single pale-pink rose in front of the headstone and then sank down to the grass to sit by Bree.

"A year."

Her voice was huskier than normal, soft and sad. He glanced at her and could tell she'd been crying. "Yeah. I can't believe it."

"Me either."

She licked her lips and glanced up at the sky. "At least it isn't pouring down rain today."

He thought back, remembered the unseasonably cold rain that had poured from the sky the day they buried Alyssa. That rain had chilled him through and through, freezing him in a way that had gone deeper than just the surface. It had frozen him clear through to the heart and he'd been grateful. He hadn't wanted to feel anything. Hadn't wanted to grieve. Grieving meant letting go and he hadn't been ready to do that.

The hot sun shone down on his back, warming him through the simple white polo shirt he'd unearthed from his closet. He could feel Bree's body heat along his side, warming him in a way the sun never could. And he could smell her—that soft, sexy scent that had nothing to do with any store-bought lotion or perfume.

She was so damn different from Alyssa. Smooth, caramel-colored skin, dark gray, quiet eyes that seemed to notice everything, a long, lean body with those dangerously sexy curves.

Aside from that pinup body, everything about Bree was subtle.

Everything about Alyssa had been vivid, intense, fast—just like her life. She had worn a riot of colors, had talked fast, jumping from one subject to the next with a speed that often left the listener struggling to keep up. Five-feet-four, a lush ripe figure, her long blondish-red hair a mass of spirals and ringlets. She'd spend nearly forty-five minutes a day on her hair, another twenty or thirty picking out her clothes and putting on makeup. Completely female. He couldn't go into the bathroom without finding something lacy and frilly and pink draped somewhere. He'd loved it. He'd loved watching her slick herself down with lotion, loved watching her mess with her hair, loved everything about her.

But he'd spent half of the last year since her death fantasizing about her best friend.

Maybe it was the polarity of the two. Bree was so damn different from Alyssa—always had been.

Or maybe you're just realizing there's an attraction there.

That thought was quickly followed by a rush of guilt. Realizing an attraction, admitting to one that had started within weeks—no, hours—of burying his wife, what kind of bastard did that make him?

It had only been hours after they'd buried Alyssa that he'd found himself lying on the floor in Bree's house, her arms around him, his head pillowed on her thigh and his mind full of her. He'd looked at her...and wanted.

So what kind of bastard was he?

The human kind? You're not dead.

"You ever think you're going stark-raving mad?" he asked abruptly.

She glanced at him. A smile tugged at her lips and she shrugged. "Daily. Sometimes hourly. Why?"

He sighed. "Just wondering."

A breeze drifted across the cemetery, bringing with it the smells of fresh earth and flowers. Bree. It wrapped around him, taunting, teasing. The memory of the voice whispering in his ear, *She's the reason you came back.*

Stupid. Fucking moronic. Why would he have come back because of Bree? She had been his wife's best friend.

Just Alyssa's friend? Not yours?

Okay, so yeah, she'd been a friend to him as well. But it was friendship. Nothing more. At least not since he'd gotten past that high-school infatuation years ago. He was a one-woman guy. He had been happy that way. Alyssa had been it for him and he had been it for her. They'd been each other's first love, each other's first lover. He'd planned on them being the only. But fate had stepped in and taken Alyssa away.

He couldn't see himself spending the rest of his life celibate. Even depressed and eaten up inside with guilt, the past year had made him all too aware that he wasn't cut out for a life without sex.

It wouldn't be too difficult, he didn't think, to get laid. A quick, anonymous fuck would ease the ache in his balls but that idea held about as much appeal as jacking off in the shower.

He wanted sex, wanted to feel a woman beneath him, her arms around him, rising to meet him as he rode her.

But he had no right wanting it from Bree.

She was his friend.

Bree said, "Colby?"

But he wasn't listening to her. It was the third time she'd said his name and he was staring off into the distance as though something out there held him spellbound.

Sighing, she pushed to her feet. Pausing by his side, she stroked a hand down his hair. Before she could walk away, though, he reached out, caught her wrist.

"Where are you going?" he asked, without looking at her.

With a shrug, she replied, "Back to work. Have a few more clients to hit before I can call it a day. Besides, you need some time to yourself, don't you?"

He lifted his head slowly, their gazes connecting. Something in her heart stuttered to a halt at the heat she saw in his eyes. Then he blinked and it was gone, as though it had never existed. "Yeah. Not a bad idea." His thumb stroked along the inner skin of her wrist. He looked as if he wanted to say something else, but what, she had no clue.

"Colby?"

He squeezed her wrist gently, then let go. "You mind if I call you in a few days? Maybe we could get a bite to eat or something."

"Sure."

When he let go, Bree felt the loss of contact clear down to her feet.

Get over it already. Get over him.

But that wasn't going to happen.

Guilty Needs

If she hadn't been able to make herself get over him as he married her best friend, she wasn't going to force herself to get over him now that Alyssa was gone.

Chapter Four

A week passed.

Two.

Three.

She didn't hear from Colby, didn't see him when she went to take care of Alyssa's flowers. By the third week, she knew he wasn't going to call and she told herself she wasn't disappointed.

She wasn't, either. Not really. As much as she might have enjoyed eating a meal with him, she didn't need to expose any more of herself to him.

So when it was time to head back out to his place, she did it during the week, figured it would be quicker, easier, if her crew went with her — the less time spent at his place the better. While her crew cut the grass and tended to the front yard, she was in the back, yanking up more of the stubborn weeds, thinning out the pansies and lilies, pruning the rose bushes.

"Bree."

Her damp hair was plastered to her forehead and she just barely managed to suppress a groan as Colby squatted down in front of her. Flicking the sweaty strands back, she glanced up at him. Her heart skipped a beat and then started doing a happy little slam-dance in her chest. He looked too damn good, too damn tempting. Guilt gnawed at her. Desire swam through her. Need, lust and love flooded her.

After fifteen years of loving him, it was second-nature to battle all of that down and give him a friendly smile. Second nature. But today, she couldn't manage it and her smile fell flat. "Hey." She focused her attention back on the rose bush, snipping away until she was satisfied.

"I'm going to get something to eat in a little while. Tired of TV dinners or soup. You want to come?"

Bree blinked. Looked down at her clothes. The gray T-shirt had been clean that morning, but after a hot day in the sun—weeding, planting, watering and everything else that went with her job—it was now far from clean. Even a kind person would have to admit that she looked grubby. Stripping off her gloves, she stood up.

Colby echoed her movement and studied her, his head cocked to the side, brow lifted in question.

"I'm not exactly dressed to get much more than a burrito from Taco Bueno." She skimmed her gaze over him, jeans and a clean black polo shirt.

His shoulders stretched against the seams of the shirt. Aside from those wide shoulders though, he looked leaner, pared down to muscle and bone. She could tell he'd lost some weight over the past year, but to her, he looked perfect. Gorgeous.

Mouth-watering.

She swallowed and hunched her shoulders, hoped the sport bra she wore would be thick enough to disguise how her nipples had gone hard the minute he said her name. Worried, she hoped she didn't start drooling—wouldn't that go well with the sweat and grime on her face?

"You look like you have something besides fast food in mind," she finished lamely, turning to collect her tools.

"I don't have much of anything in mind except a decent hot meal." He glanced at the truck in the driveway and said, "Your guys rode over with you?"

"Yeah."

"Then let them take the truck back. I'll drive you home and you can shower. Then we can get something." He gave her the smile that had been melting her heart since her freshman year of high school. "You're not going to make me eat alone, are you?"

If she had a lick of sense, yes, she would have, Bree decided an hour and half later as she locked herself inside her bathroom. The cool air conditioning was a kiss on her sweaty, overheated face and she stripped out of her clothes and just let it wash over her for a few minutes.

Colby was out in her living room. She tried to ignore her body's instinctive response, the way her heartbeat skipped, the way her belly heated, the way her nipples went tight and hard and her sex wet and achy.

He was out there waiting.

Waiting for her.

A nice, friendly meal, she reminded herself, trying to cool the need raging inside her. She could handle a nice friendly meal. Sure.

She could do—

"Why does it have to be friendly?"

Alyssa's voice startled her. Out of the blue and responding to something that Bree hadn't said out loud. Narrowing her eyes, she searched the bathroom and saw nothing. A second sweep of the room ended up revealing Alyssa's transparent form perched atop the bathroom counter, swinging her feet and watching Bree with a sly smile. "Do you have to do that?" she demanded, keeping her voice down.

Alyssa's smile widened. "Do what?"

"Pop in and out like that."

Alyssa shrugged. "Sorry. Can't get used to this whole ghost deal. I thought you knew I was here."

"You need a cow bell." Turning her heel, she moved to the shower and leaned it to adjust the spray.

"And you didn't answer me. Why does it have to be friendly?"

"Why can't you just let this go?"

"Because I'm stubborn?"

Bree snorted. Stubborn. Okay. Pit bulls were stubborn, latching onto something and never, ever letting go. Alyssa was worse than that. "Not you," she said, her voice mocking. "Stubborn?"

Alyssa lifted a brow. "No more stubborn than you. You've loved him half your life and don't try to make me think otherwise. You never lied to me, don't start now," she warned, wagging her finger in Bree's direction.

Blood rushed to her cheeks and she clamped her lips shut against the automatic denial that tried to come out. No point in lying about it, right?

But judging by the look on Alyssa's face, she heard Bree's thoughts as clearly as if she'd said them. Her best friend's eyes narrowed and Bree glared right back. "Don't go snarling at me, damn it. It ain't my fault you went and got frickin' telepathic on me. I'm allowed to think whatever I want to think."

Alyssa's irritated gaze faded away, replaced by one that wasn't any easier to face. Sympathy. Hell, Bree hated anybody feeling sorry for her. "Of course you're allowed to think what you want...and I'm sorry. If I could figure out a way to turn this off, I would. But it's like...I dunno, some weird radio that tunes itself in and out and I don't have much control over it." She glanced toward the floor, as though she could see right through and see Colby down there.

He'd be pacing, Bree knew. Or getting a drink from her fridge, then pacing. The two of them together—Alyssa and Colby—had been like being around a live wire at times. Colby moved at a slower pace than Alyssa ever had but there was still a vague restlessness to it, as if he was thinking of other things nonstop and movement helped him deal with all those other things.

"He thinks of you. No matter what you think, that means something," Alyssa said quietly.

"I doubt it. I don't think it means much of anything," Bree said. But there was a knot in her chest.

"And if you're wrong? What if it means everything?"

Alyssa sighed and turned away. Her transparent body wavered in and out of focus and Bree knew from experience that she was fading and when she disappeared it would be a few days before she saw her friend again.

What if it means everything?

"I don't believe in what-ifs, Alyssa."

But Alyssa was already gone, leaving Bree alone in the room with Alyssa's words rising to haunt her.

What if it means everything?

So what?

Alyssa said he thought about her. That could mean anything. Could be nothing. Before the ghost of Alyssa's voice started to whisper any louder, Bree climbed into the shower, letting the pouring water drive away all conscious thought.

* * * * *

When the shower kicked on upstairs, Colby headed down to the basement on the pretense of going through Bree's wine. It was as far as he could get from the bathroom without leaving the house.

He didn't have to hear the water to get caught thinking about it, though. Just knowing she was taking a shower brought to mind images of her standing under the spray, that long, golden body naked and slick, water sluicing down over her shoulders, between her breasts, along the flat plane of her belly, beads of water catching in the curls that covered her pussy.

And immediately, his body reacted, his blood kicking up to a low boil and his cock swelling until he had to adjust himself. Fuck, he hurt. Just the touch of his own hand was pure agony. His balls ached something vicious.

You need to get laid.

Last week, he'd left the house with just that intention in mind. It had ended up a waste of time. He'd gone down to the strip, settled at the bar with a Jack and Coke. Within five minutes, a pretty blue-eyed redhead had settled down next to him, but for all her flirting, Colby had absolutely no interest in her.

They danced, they shared a meal, they walked along the strip, but when she invited him back to her place, Colby had no desire to go. He could have done it. After more than a year without a woman, he knew he could have gone back to her place and spent the next four hours fucking her, but it wouldn't mean anything.

Colby needed it to mean something. He didn't know what that made him. Plenty of guys he knew, both from before Alyssa's illness and after her death, were just fine with quick, anonymous sex. But Colby wasn't into it and he wasn't going to get laid just so he could spend the next few weeks feeling guilty.

He had enough to feel guilty about already.

His skin tightened. Goose bumps broke out. Hissing out from between his teeth, he turned around just as the voice started to whisper. Alyssa's voice.

Squeezing his eyes closed, he tried to pull up a mental image of her. He could still remember the sound of her voice, but unless he looked at a picture, his memory of her seemed to grow fuzzier every day.

"There's nothing for you to feel guilty about, baby."

Baby?

Cracking one eye open, he glanced around the room. He wouldn't call himself baby, not even if he was creating the voice out of deep guilt, need and loneliness. Was he really—

No. No, he wasn't really hearing her voice.

"How come you're so certain of that?"

Usually, he managed to not answer these kinds of questions. But this time, the answer leaped out before he could stop it. "I'm not really hearing you because you're dead."

The words sounded so damn harsh, he flinched when he heard them.

But she laughed.

It wrapped around him, warm and soothing. "Yeah, I'm dead. But since when did you stop believing in ghosts, Colby?"

"Ghosts." He shook his head, turning in a slow circle around the room, eyeing the dark corners for wispy, insubstantial figures, balls of light, something. "Why should I believe that my dead wife is a ghost?"

"Same reason any dead person becomes a ghost. Unfinished business. Do you see me, Colby? Can you? Do you want to?"

"I can't see you." He slapped a hand against his temple, muttered, "You need to snap out of it."

"Why can't you see me? Don't you want to?"

"Yes." Simply, flatly stated. Yes. He wanted to see Alyssa.

And then he did. At first, he couldn't quite believe what he was seeing as she shimmered into view, looking as she had before she'd gotten sick, the picture of vitality and life, except he could see right through her. "Lyssie?"

She smiled at him. "Hi, baby."

Colby could explain away voices. He had an active imagination, he'd lost his wife, he had wet dreams about her best friend—all sorts of stuff that would make a shrink very happy indeed. But he was also pretty damn logical and always had been. Explaining away voices was a lot easier than explaining away the fact that his wife was standing in front of him, wearing her favorite sundress, her hair falling in wild corkscrews all over the place and she was transparent.

Not so easy to explain away.

Voice gritty, he asked, "Are you real?"

Alyssa shrugged. "What is real? Am I here talking to you? Yeah. Am I really a ghost? Yeah." Then she reached out and laid a hand on his chest.

He could feel it—a cold spot, just above his heart.

"But you can't touch me. I can't really touch you," she finished, her voice sad and quiet.

"You really have been talking to me."

"Yes." She grinned and her voice was exasperated as she said, "Baby, you ignored me for months, ya know. Or just rationalized it away. I'm starting to think you should have gone into politics, the way you explain things away."

Sarcastically, he muttered, "Well, gee, thanks."

Alyssa drifted away from him, not exactly walking, but not really hovering the way he would have thought a ghost would. It was almost like something tugged her away as she said, "I always thought Bree was stubborn."

Bree.

The sound of her name had his guilt dropping down like a stone albatross around his neck, dragging him under. Blood rushed to his face and then drained away as nausea churned inside him. "Bree..."

"Why do you feel so guilty, Colby? It's not like you left me for her. I'm gone. For good. I'm only here to make sure you're going to be okay and then that's it. So why do you feel so guilty for needing her?"

Needing her? He didn't—

But all his dreams over the past six months rose up to haunt him, defying him. And Alyssa stood there watching him with knowing eyes. "Why don't you want to need her?"

"I made a promise to you. I swore to love you. I don't want to love anybody else."

"Not really something we can control." Alyssa sighed. Her body shimmered, wavered with the sound, before solidifying again until she seemed almost solid. "You did make a promise...and you kept it. You promised to love me 'til death do us part...then death parted us. You're free from that promise."

"And if I don't want to be?"

Her eyes flashed. The room chilled. Abruptly, Colby remembered other times when he'd heard this voice, the irritation or anger, followed by an icy chill. It was her—came from her—he realized.

"What are you going to do, spend your life alone?" she demanded. "Is that what you want?"

"I want my wife back!" he shouted. His voice echoed around him, the words leaving an empty, aching hole in his chest. "I need my wife back."

"No. You don't."

Alyssa reached out, her hand hovering just above his cheek. He could feel the cold radiating off her and it made him think of Bree. Made him think of her warmth. Her smile.

As though she knew exactly what he was thinking, Alyssa nodded. "You need her. More, you want her. It's time to let me go, baby. Letting me go doesn't mean you don't love me. It just means you're ready to love her."

"Bree." He shook his head. "I don't love her. I..."

Alyssa smiled at him. "Don't you?"

"It doesn't happen like that."

She gave him a quick wink as she backed away. "Love doesn't have a rulebook, you know. It can happen any way it wants." Her words hadn't even faded in the air before she was gone.

If Bree hadn't come looking for him, Colby had no idea how long he might have stayed down there in the basement, staring at nothing, replaying those minutes with Alyssa over and over and over—each word, each movement.

Letting me go doesn't mean you don't love me — it just means you're ready to love her.

I don't love her.

Don't you?

Like a DVD stuck and skipping back to the last scene, he kept going back to that.

It just means you're ready to love her.

I don't love her.

"Colby?"

Her quiet voice drifted down the stairs and he closed his eyes. For a few minutes, he'd almost forgotten where he was. "Yeah, I'm down here," he said, raising his voice just a little.

At the sound of her feet moving lightly down the stairs, he turned. She glanced at him, then down. He realized he was still holding a bottle of wine. "Sorry. I was thinking about getting a drink."

She shrugged. "I don't mind." As she moved closer, he caught the scent of soap and lotion—something exotic, like coconut and tropical flowers. "We can have a glass before we go eat if you want." She took the bottle from him and turned it until she could read the label.

A glass? Oh. Yeah. Wine.

Not for him, really. He'd given up on alcohol. He'd come down here to distract himself so he wasn't thinking about a wet, naked Bree. And he'd ended up being confronted by his wife, who really didn't care if he was thinking about a wet, naked Bree.

Getting a drink was the last thing on his mind but he couldn't exactly tell her he'd given up on drinking when looking for a bottle of wine sounded so much better than the truth.

Sorry, came down here so I wasn't thinking about you wet and naked in the shower.

Well, no, not exactly right—Alyssa did care, as in she wanted to have him thinking about Bree. In any capacity. Wet. Naked. Clothed.

"Changed my mind," he said, his voice rusty. "We can, though, if you want."

Bree just shrugged. "Nah. I'm better off getting something to eat first. Skipped lunch. A glass of wine will probably go straight to my head right now."

Oh, now that was just not what he needed to hear. A tipsy Bree, her hair still damp from the shower and her skin smelling of tropical flowers and Colby on a mission to track down just where the scent was the strongest. Her neck? Along her torso? Lower?

Suppressing a groan, he took the bottle and returned it to the shelves. "Let's head on out then."

Before he decided to open that bottle and drag Bree to the shower, because just then, a wet, naked, tipsy Bree sounded like bliss.

* * * * *

"Are you okay?"

Colby glanced up from his lasagna to smile at her. It was a familiar one, the one that said he was distracted, thinking about ten different things and not really paying attention. But when she had been about ready to repeat herself, he'd shrugged. "Yeah, I'm fine. Just…do you believe in ghosts?"

She'd been lifting her sweet tea up for a drink, but as that question hung in the air between them, she lowered it back to the table and then ended up folding her hands in her lap. "Ghosts?"

He nodded.

"Yeah." Squirming on the bench, with its thin cushion and hard back, she met his gaze and nodded. "I believe in ghosts. Not necessarily the kind that rattle chains or play with the lights, but I believe in them. Sometimes people die before they can take care of everything they wanted to do."

"Unfinished business," he murmured.

A shiver raced down Bree's spine as he echoed the words Alyssa had said to her so many times.

"I..." he licked his lips, leaned back in his chair and crossed his arms over his chest. The material of his shirt drew tight across his biceps and shoulders and for a second, Bree was too distracted to follow him. Then she heard him say Alyssa's name. "Would she have any reason to come back? She wasn't exactly the type to start and not finish something."

Except me, Bree thought ruefully. *I'm her latest and last project.* "Sometimes they don't have much choice." She didn't want to ask him. It was too damn weird.

But she couldn't not ask. "Is this about Alyssa?"

She could see the answer in his eyes. He'd seen her. When, though?

She might have even asked him, except, just like that, his features became shuttered, blank. With a shake of his head, he muttered, "No. Forget I said anything."

The rest of the meal passed in awkward silence and Bree ended up leaving two-thirds of her spaghetti uneaten on her plate. By the time the waitress came with the check, she was damn anxious to get out of there and apparently Colby was in the same state of mind. They both reached for the check at the same time. "I'll take care of mine," she said.

He didn't even look at her. "I brought you. I'll pay."

Arguing with him was only going to keep them trapped there longer and she needed to get out of there, get away from him.

He'd locked her out.

Again.

The pain inside him was a cancer and all she wanted to do was help, but he wouldn't let her. He had disappeared for a year, no letters, no phone calls, nothing—it was pretty damn clear he didn't want or need her help.

In her chest, her heart was a cold, icy knot. *He doesn't want me, Lys. I wish you could see that.*

The drive to her house was another exercise in awkward, tense silences, but when she tried to make her escape, he hit the door locks just as she reached for the handle. "I'm sorry. I think I forgot how to act with people in public," he said quietly. Sliding her a glance, he shrugged. "It's been a weird day."

"They happen." She wanted to lean forward and wrap her arms around his shoulders. His eyes were so serious and he looked so worried, so miserable. But touching him? Not a good idea.

Instead, she forced a smile and said, "Don't worry about it."

Don't worry about it? Oh, the irony.

For the next week, Colby did nothing but worry about it. Worry about her. Worry about Alyssa. Worry about the very weird day when he'd seen his wife's ghost in the basement of her best friend's house.

She hadn't made a return appearance.

Even when he had another dream about Bree and woke up feeling sick with guilt. It had hit him hard, but instead of collapsing under it, he'd shoved back. "There's nothing to feel guilty about," he'd told himself. He mostly even believed it. At least now.

And that might be why Alyssa hadn't made a repeat appearance.

He spent the week in his office going through paperwork. On Friday, he found a partially finished manuscript that he'd set aside probably four years earlier. Most of his stuff was in the urban fantasy scene, with a few more traditional pieces.

Darkness might have some urban fantasy aspects, but it was too dark, too macabre to be called anything but horror. Flipping through the loose pages, he found himself getting engrossed. A red pen, a tepid bottle of water—with his back pressed against the wall, he lost track of time, making notes in the margin, going back, rewriting a few passages in long hand then he got to the last page and realized the sun had set and he'd spent the past four hours doing rewrites on a piece that wasn't even done.

But the story had turned into a song in his head, one that wouldn't shut up. So instead of stretching out the kinks in his back and getting something to silence the growl in his belly, he pulled out the chair, booted up the computer and brought up the file holding the notes and partial manuscript for *Darkness*.

By the time the song in his head settled down to a quiet hum, it was dark outside. Dark in his office too, because he'd never bothered to turn on the lights. He didn't bother doing so now, either. Instead, he just saved the updated file and made a backup copy on an SD card he found buried in one of the drawers.

His back was a mess of knots and aches. Exhaustion pushed at him but he didn't head to the guest room where he'd been sleeping since he came home.

He headed outside, stripping out of his clothes, his goal the pool.

It had hit the high nineties today and right now, he'd bet the water would feel like warm silk. He was right. The water closed over him in an embrace. Holding his breath, he swam along the bottom until he had to surface. Then he started to swim laps.

His muscles warmed and he fell into a regular rhythm. Letting his mind drift, he toyed with the plotline for *Darkness*, taking mental notes and debating whether or not he should even try getting a proposal together for his agent. Hell, if she was still his agent. He hadn't talked to her in a year and he wouldn't be surprised if she'd decided to let him go. Yeah, he'd made her a decent amount of money but he was dead weight right now. Publishing didn't allow for a lot of dead weight.

But the story wasn't going quiet—he already knew that. He even had a glimmer of how it was going to end and unless he'd lost his rhythm during his twelve-month break away from the computer, he had a feeling he could wrap *Darkness* up in a few weeks.

Putting together a proposal was a good idea.

His muscles were starting to burn but he didn't quit swimming until he'd managed to hammer out the basics in his mind and formulate a somewhat formal letter to his agent. Angela Browning wasn't the overly formal type, but since he'd been playing mute the past year, going formal wasn't a bad idea.

He swam another two laps and then just let his body float.

Overhead, the moon shone down—a pure, clear circle of silvery-white. His mind drifted, with little surprise, to Bree.

It just means you're ready to love her.

Ready to love Bree.

For some reason, the idea of it didn't rub him quite so raw. Ready. Was he ready?

Always one to test himself, Colby deliberately thought about his wife. For the longest time after she'd died, he wouldn't let himself think about her and when he had, he'd tried to jerk his thoughts away before he got lost in them. Thinking about her bought a stab of pain that threatened to eviscerate him.

It got to be habit, until he found himself thinking intentionally less and less. Wayward thoughts would intrude and he'd find himself fighting the tidal wave of grief, but thinking back, he realized that had been slowly ebbing down over the past couple of months.

It no longer had the power to level him.

And now? It was the first time he'd deliberately tried to do much more than visualize her face in his mind—excluding all the times he'd done it just to punish himself.

He went through a mental list, tried to recall the way she smelled. The way she tasted. The way she felt against him. It was all too hazy and vague. A surreal memory that would grow ever fainter with every passing day. Some part of him hated that—he wanted to keep her memory alive. But, even as he tried to make his thoughts of Alyssa clearer, more vivid, he realized other thoughts were trying to intrude.

Bree.

He closed his eyes, and just like that, he could see her. The way she knelt in the grass, her long, slender fingers digging through the earth. The way she smelled of flowers and sunshine. The smooth, golden glow of her skin and the quiet, deep gray of her eyes. Her smile. The way one look at her had his knees going weak while his dick got hard.

It just means you're ready to love her.

Maybe.

Just maybe.

Of course, just because he was ready to admit that maybe he was falling in love with Bree didn't mean she felt the same.

And one thing he knew he wasn't ready for was to have his heart shatter inside his chest again.

Chapter Five

Saturday dawned a little cooler, the skies a leaden shade of gray and threatening rain. Although Bree tended to sleep in a little on weekends, she rolled out of bed and hit the shower. Saturday—she needed to cut some flowers from the backyard and take them to Alyssa.

It was a ritual.

After a quick shower, she cut a couple of stargazer lilies from one of her flowerbeds in the back, their pale petals streaked with deep pink. She wrapped the stems in wet paper towels and climbed into her truck—only to swear, the second she looked at the gas gauge.

She'd forgotten to fill up. If she took the truck, she might not have enough gas to make the drive to the cemetery. Weird for her, but the past few weeks had been a study in weirdness. So much so that she couldn't do more than sigh and swear under her breath as she climbed out and headed for her bike.

Half an hour later, she knelt by Alyssa's grave and took out the flowers she'd brought last week, replacing them with the fresh lilies. They'd fared okay on the bike ride, she guessed. Good thing she hadn't decided to bring roses this time.

"So are you still going to be bringing me flowers this time next year? Five years down the road?"

Blowing a sigh, Bree looked up to see Alyssa sitting on the stone bench a few feet away. "You know, it's sort of a respect thing."

Alyssa shrugged. "No. It's sort of a comfort thing people do for their loved ones." Her face softened with a smile and she said, "I'm glad you still think about me, but you don't need to bring flowers to do that."

"I'll bring flowers if I want to bring flowers."

Alyssa's dimples appeared. "Which means, knowing you, you'll still be hobbling down to my grave when you're ninety, just to bring me flowers."

"So what if I do?" Tears stung her eyes. Ninety — hell, was she really going to be still doing this in sixty years? Spending her nights alone, making Saturday treks to a cemetery to sit with a friend who never should have died so young?

"If I wasn't meant to die so young, Bree, I wouldn't have died."

Feeling more than a little bitchy, Bree snapped, "Are you still going to be fussing at me for bringing you flowers when I'm ninety?"

But the expected retort didn't come. She looked at Alyssa and found her friend gazing at her with something between grief and peace. "No. I don't think I'm going to be fussing at you much more at all."

Bree blinked. "Huh?"

Alyssa shifted her gaze, staring at a point behind Bree. "I still love him, you know. And if it was anybody but you, I think this would hurt like hell."

"What are you talking about?"

Alyssa smiled. Her body shimmered, faded. "I love you, Bree. You were the best friend any girl could have ever wanted. Be happy with him."

"Are we back to that?" Bree demanded.

But the question was posed to empty air, because Alyssa was already gone.

She didn't know what made her turn.

She hadn't heard his car, hadn't heard him approach and she knew he hadn't said anything. But he was there. She knew it even before she turned around. Slowly, her legs stiff, her heart slamming away, she turned to watch as Colby walked her way.

There was something different about him.

It had only been a week since she'd seen him, but something had changed. She couldn't quite put her finger on it.

His hair was still too long, in desperate need of a cut. He looked a little tanner, like he'd spent some time working outside. But that wasn't it. He moved... She nibbled on her lip, watched how he strode toward her and thought back.

His walk, she realized.

The past few weeks and before, really back when Alyssa and he had first gotten the news that the cancer was too advanced, he had walked as though he had the weight of the world crushing down on him.

Slow. Not feeble or anything. Just deliberately slow, as though, if he moved too fast, the weight on his shoulders would fall and crash. Or he would.

As if he were doing some sort of unseen balancing act.

But that had changed.

He moved with the confident, easy grace he'd been born with.

He came, halted beside her and smiled, reached up to brush her bangs back from her eyes. He glanced at the flowers on Alyssa's grave, then down at the ones he held. It was a store-bought bouquet, a bunch of daisies that were dyed brilliant colors. They looked exactly like something Alyssa would have loved.

"Yours look better than mine," he said.

Bree made herself smile and shrug. "Yeah, but yours look like something Alyssa would have picked out." She took them from him and knelt, under the pretense of adding his daises in with her lilies. Really, she mostly needed to have a minute to get her breathing level before he wondered why she was practically panting.

The daisies' bright colors should have looked silly next to the quiet beauty of the lilies, but she decided it looked just right. "How are you doing?"

"Good. I think." He crouched down beside her. From the corner of her eye, she glanced at him and saw that he was smiling. The faint, easy sort of smile a person had when things were going right. An unconscious smile. "Was going through my office yesterday and found an old story I'd set aside. Ended up flipping through it and next thing I know, it's nine o'clock, I've added fifty pages to the story and half the plot is worked out."

"Really? That's great." She turned to look at him, smiling. He hadn't written anything since he'd finished the last book in his contract a month before Alyssa died. "Your agent is going to be thrilled."

He grimaced. "If she still wants to be my agent. I've left her hanging for quite a while."

Without realizing what she was doing, she leaned forward and hugged him. "You've had a hell of a lot to deal with, Colby. She'll understand that." She squeezed, but before she could pull away, his arms came up and wrapped around her.

It was an awkward position, her kneeling, Colby balanced on his heels. But he didn't seem interested in letting her go. Bree didn't have the will to pull back from him, not even when he shifted around and settled on the ground so he could pull her into his lap. All without letting go. "I missed you," he said quietly, his breath whispering along her skin.

It was an innocent statement.

Even his embrace was innocent. Bree knew that.

Just as she knew, if she didn't get away from him soon, she was going to embarrass herself. She squeezed him and said, "I know. I missed you too." Then she tried to ease back.

He let her, but he didn't let go completely. She ended up sitting on the ground between his thighs, one of his hands on her waist. She sat as straight as she could, trying to keep from leaning against him. "Where did you spend the past year?" she asked, trying to make herself think about something other than the fact that he was so damn close.

"Here...there...everywhere. Spent some time in South Carolina, drove down the coast. Spent the past couple of months working in Mobile." He shrugged.

"Doing what?"

"Nothing at first. Just driving. Had to keep moving around. Made it easier for a while. I took some money from my savings account and just used it for hotels, to eat on. When it was gone, I sold the Lexus and bought the cheapest car I could find and just did more driving around. Worked odd jobs—bartending, construction, whatever."

"Did it help?"

He was silent for a while. When he answered, his voice was thoughtful, slow, as though he still wasn't entirely sure of the answer. "I don't know. Some, I think. I hid from it for a while. Hid from her dying. Did my damnedest not to think about her if I could, and when I started to think about her, I made myself stop. It made it easier."

"You weren't ready." Shifting around, she knelt in front of him.

He lifted a hand and cupped her face.

The feel of him touching her almost had her shuddering and she just barely managed to throttle it down. But she couldn't control everything, and when she spoke, her voice was low and raspy. That could be blamed on other things though. He didn't have to know it was because she was dying for him, right? "Sometimes we're just not ready to deal with things. The mind shields us until we are, gives us time. You just needed some time. It gets easier."

"Yeah." He slid his hand down, cupped it over the back of her neck. An unconscious gesture, she suspected, as he focused his dark amber gaze on Alyssa's gravestone. "I'm going to love her for the rest of my life."

Her heart broke. It was amazing that he didn't hear the way it cracked inside her chest, amazing she didn't drop lifeless to his feet as it shattered into thousands of useless pieces. "I know you will."

His gaze came back to her then and her useless, shattered heart trembled at the look in his eyes. But it was just a fantasy. He couldn't really be looking at her like that. Looking at her with something an awful lot like desire — and more.

Just a fantasy, she told herself as the sound of cars approaching broke the silence and ended the weird tension in the air. As one, they turned their heads, watched as a funeral procession turned off the main road into the cemetery. He stood and held out a hand. "I don't really want to hang around here for this. Do you?"

She grimaced. "Not especially." Tracking the line of cars with her eyes, she slid him a glance. "Are you parked there?"

"Yeah. Maybe we could get something to eat and you could bring me to get my car later."

"I'm on my bike." She glanced up at the sky, but to her surprise, the leaden gray clouds were clearing up and sun was starting to stream through.

Colby shrugged. "I don't care."

"I don't have an extra helmet."

"I don't care."

Bree opened her mouth to say something else. Then she glanced back at the funeral procession and the unending line of cars. Alyssa's funeral had been like that, attended by so many people that the parking lots had overflowed. If they were going to leave, it needed to be soon.

Five minutes later, he mounted the bike behind her, rested his hands on her waist as she started it up. Already, cars were heading their way, coming around the back road toward the smaller parking lot. Bree whipped out of there before the first of the cars made it halfway down the lane.

Heat.

Shit, the heat of her was going to kill him. Even if guilt decided to rear its ugly head and make him suffer for what he was thinking, the heat would kill him before guilt had a chance.

The vibrations of the bike rumbled through him and he sat plastered against the long, slender line of her back. Involuntarily, his hands tightened on her waist and he had to consciously relax them. Worse, his body reacted to the nearness of hers and he knew there was no way in hell he could hide it.

Maybe she wouldn't notice.

And maybe it was snowing in hell at that very moment. His dick ached, his entire body was drawn tight and all he could think about was getting her to pull the bike over and turn to face him.

He didn't know what the hell he was doing—well, that was wrong. He did know what he was doing, though he hadn't planned on starting it here. *Great timing, slick. Make a move on her at the cemetery.* But he hadn't exactly made a move on her. He'd just done what felt right. Colby had been with one woman for more than half his life—back when other guys were learning to deliver lines, he'd been focused on one girl—just one. He'd never spent any time learning whatever rules went along with dating and shit, because he'd never had to. He knew the rules of courtesy, because his mother had drummed them into him.

But dating? Flirting? No. Doing what seemed right was all he knew.

And this—riding on the back of Bree's bike with her slender back pressed close to him—seemed right.

Minutes sped by as she took the winding road farther into the hills, away from the small country cemetery and even farther away from the sprawl of the city. He had an idea where she was headed. She confirmed it a few minutes later, slowing for a light as they neared the small town roughly fifteen miles away from the cemetery. Over her shoulder, she said, "I thought we could just go to the winery and grab a sandwich at the café. Kill an hour or so. That work?"

An hour. He could think of a better way to kill an hour.

Damn it, get your brain away from your dick, he told himself, disgusted. But then he heard it again. Alyssa's soft, certain whisper.

She's the reason you came back...

"Works for me."

He felt too good behind her. Bree knew she needed to get off the bike and get some distance between them, and the winery was the closest place to eat that she could think of, other than her house, and she sure as hell wasn't taking him there. Every damn mile had been an exercise in frustrated longing, one she didn't need. Considering she'd been lusting after the guy for more than half her life, she knew all about frustrated longing and needed no refreshers, thank you very much.

But that was what she got.

He spent the entire twenty-five minutes pressed up close and personal with her. Riding on a bike made little room for personal space, but even when she had slowed for the stop sign a few minutes back, had he taken a few seconds to shift away?

No.

Being pressed up close and personal obviously doesn't affect him the way it affects you, her common sense pointed out.

Except her body could tell otherwise.

She had felt it, the way he'd reacted, his body getting hotter and hotter until it seemed like the air around them should spontaneously combust. The way his hands had tightened around her waist for the briefest second, as if he wanted to tug her even closer, though that didn't seem possible. She sped down the road to the winery, following the winding twists and turns and trying to focus on them. He dominated her thoughts, though.

The thick, hard length of his cock burned through their clothes, snug against her butt and lower back. *Unaffected? Hell, no.* She could feel the rhythmic pulse of his penis, and to her horror, her body responded in kind—her nipples throbbing, her pussy aching. All from a fucking twenty-five minute ride.

Parking in the lot adjacent to the café, Bree waited for him to climb off so she could get a little distance between them.

But Colby took his time.

Way too much time.

Sliding off, his hands lingering on her waist before falling away and, instead of taking a few steps away and giving her some room, he stood right there, practically at her shoulder. Her fingers shook as she fumbled with her helmet and she swore under her breath. Before climbing off, she sucked in a couple of deep breaths, hoping it would clear her head a little.

It might have worked. If he hadn't been standing so close that she all but tripped over him as she climbed off her bike. Even knowing how close he was, even taking extreme care not to touch him, she stumbled into him. His hands came up, caught her upper arms, steadied her—and lingered. Heart pounding, she lifted her gaze and met his, saw the dark gold depths glinting like hot, molten gold. Her vision narrowed as his gaze roamed her face, lingering on her mouth. Her lips buzzed, almost as though he'd dipped his head and kissed her.

Before she could do anything more to make a fool of herself, he let go.

As he walked away from her, she whispered a silent prayer of thanks.

She could get through this. An hour, ninety minutes, tops, then she could get him back to the cemetery—fuck, another ride on the bike with him—and then leave him alone, go home and crawl into a hot shower and hope she could ease the greedy lust that threatened to overwhelm her.

She could get through this.

Bree continued to tell herself that every few minutes as they walked to the café and placed an order. By the time the food was delivered, she even halfway believed it. Out of desperation, she'd asked Colby more about the story he'd been working on. It was one guaranteed way to get him talking so she could focus on the task of getting herself together.

When he talked about writing, he got animated. She could all but see the way it was unfolding for him. Sometime during his response, she managed to relax, even managed, just barely, to quit clenching her knees together with the hope of easing the empty ache inside her.

Yeah. She could get through this.

But then they finished eating and started back outside.

Right when they got to her bike, as she started to wrap up her personal pep talk, Colby turned to her. Bree was reaching for her helmet, but he caught her wrist. With a faint smile on her face, she lifted her eyes to his. The smile died, though, at the look on his face.

"If I did something I probably shouldn't do, would you forgive me?" he asked, rubbing his thumb along the sensitive skin of her inner wrist.

"Ah...I guess that would depend on what the 'something' is."

His voice was gruff and low. "This." He let go of her wrist and used both hands to cup her face and tilt her head back. Then he kissed her.

Not some friendly peck on the cheek, either.

His tongue pushed inside her mouth, delving deep. Her knees buckled and she instinctively brought her hands up, wrapped them around his wrists to steady herself. It was a waste of energy though—nothing could steady her. They barely touched, his mouth on hers, his hands cupping her face while hers clutched at his wrists. But that contact was enough to shatter the foundation of her world.

He eased up, lifted his head just a little. An involuntary whimper escaped her and she swayed toward him. He growled low in his throat and reached for her, hauling her against him until they were plastered together. Her breasts pressed flat against the muscled wall of his chest and his cock cuddled against the mound of her sex.

He took her mouth again, tracing the outline of her lips with his tongue before pushing inside. One hand stroked down her side, his fingers grazing the outer curve of her breast, then down, down, down, until he could palm her ass. He did so, drawing her closer and holding her steady as he pumped against her.

She shuddered in response. Her pussy went hot and slick with need, aching, yearning to feel him inside her. Her nipples stabbed into his chest—burning hot, swollen, sensitive.

She needed more. That was all she could think. She needed *more*.

Everything.

Fisting her hands in his shirt, she rocked to meet him. Whimpered. Might have even begged, if he hadn't been feasting on her mouth as though he were starved for the taste of her.

She might have even believed he was. If she believed in fairy tales.

A car horn blared, shattering the silence. She jerked, would have torn away from him if he had let her. Panicked, she stared up at him. Colby returned her gaze levelly, lifting a hand to cup her cheek. "That's the something," he whispered roughly.

But her mind couldn't quite process his comment.

Guilty Needs

Her mind had stopped working, and if he hadn't closed his fingers around her wrist and helped her climb on the bike, she might have just stood there indefinitely.

Stood there on legs that trembled while her body ached for his and her mind spun around in dizzying, confusing circles.

She wanted to ask him why. Why had he kissed her like that? He took her helmet, put it in her hands but she couldn't quite get her hands to work the helmet.

Colby ended up taking it from her, sliding it on her head and fastening the chin strap. Bree was pretty damn sure her brain had short-circuited on her. She barely even remembered him taking the keys from her and mounting the bike — a feat that took some skill because he climbed on in front of her.

Her body slid forward to press against his. Now *that* she could remember.

The heat of his body, the muscled line of his back and thighs so close to her own. Overheated brain or not, she'd have to be dead to not remember the way he felt.

But even the ride home passed in a blur. A fogged, aroused blur where every breath was both heaven and hell because she could feel the strength of his body pressed against her own, where the vibrations of the bike rocked through her, and each small shift had her panties rubbing against her swollen clit. It was one hot, aroused blur.

She didn't remember getting home. She did remember him walking her through the garage, pausing at the door to press his lips to hers one last time — light and quick — before he locked the door behind him. None of it registered until she heard the rumble of her bike once more.

On watery legs, she made her way to the front of the house and watched through the picture window as he rode off.

Abruptly, her brain turned back on and she started to shake. Her legs gave out beneath her and she collapsed to the floor. Drawing her knees to her chest, she pressed her overheated face against them while her mind replayed the past two hours.

Colby had kissed her.

Colby had kissed her.

She licked her lips and she didn't know if it was remnant need or just her imagination but it seemed like she could taste him. Her body buzzed as though he still held her tightly against him. Her nipples burned, her pussy throbbed—she was so aroused, she hurt with it. Need could be so very painful.

Falling back onto the hardwood floor, she lay there, shaking, sweating and confused. Her body screamed at her. She was pretty damn sure, if Colby appeared right then and there and just looked at her the right way, she'd come. She needed it—hell, but did she need it. Briefly, she thought about trying to get upright and stumble into the shower. A massaging showerhead made for one hell of a tension reliever, but she discarded the idea almost as quickly as it formed.

It wouldn't work. Not this time.

Bree wasn't too certain that anything short of getting very naked, very hot and very sweaty with Colby would work. A few hours ago, her mind would have discarded even the possibility of that. Although she still remembered in vivid detail those few tense, heated moments right in her kitchen a year ago—remembered the hunger she'd glimpsed in his eyes—she knew he hadn't really needed anything more than comfort that day. The kind of comfort he'd needed might have ripped her heart out, but she would have given it.

But now…he hadn't been looking for comfort.

Bree recognized a man on the make easy enough, even if she hadn't ever seen it coming from him. That was all it was, she just couldn't believe it was anything deeper than that, no matter how much she wanted it. He needed a woman.

Alyssa had been gone a year, and deep inside, Bree knew that Colby hadn't been with a woman since his wife had become too ill. He needed sex.

But Bree needed him and she wasn't so certain her heart could handle it if he'd decided, for some fucked up reason, to end his sexual fast with her.

Chapter Six

His hands were sweating.

Ever since he'd driven away from Bree three hours earlier, he'd been in a persistent state of arousal and he hadn't thought much of anything would ease the burning ache in his balls. Well, anything short of stripping Bree naked and fucking her until she screamed herself hoarse. That would work. At least until he needed to do it again.

But he'd been wrong—there was one thing that could douse the fire burning inside him.

Why it happened then, he didn't know. It wasn't that he consciously made the decision that he needed to let go of Alyssa. It wasn't as if he hadn't admitted his attraction to her best friend—an attraction that he realized had probably always been there. It wasn't one he ever would have acted on, maybe not even one he would ever have been consciously aware of, if life hadn't tossed him one major sucker punch and taken Alyssa from him.

He'd loved his wife. He still did. He never would have broken the promises he made her.

But sometime since he'd let himself acknowledge the fact that—okay, still not easy to think it—Alyssa was haunting him, he'd realized why she'd been doing so. He hadn't died with her. Even though there had been weeks where he wished he had, he hadn't. He was still alive.

And she hated how he'd shut down. She loved him enough, even though she was gone, to want him to be happy. She knew him enough to know who could make him happy.

He'd thought maybe he could get past the guilt.

Then he found himself standing in front of the door to their room. The room he'd shared with Alyssa—the room where he'd held her in his arms as she quietly passed away in her sleep.

He hadn't gone in there once since he'd returned home. He didn't want to go in there.

But he couldn't turn away either. He inched forward, one slow, shuffling step at a time, and every step he took, memories flashed through his mind. Alyssa as she had looked on their wedding day. Bree standing in the rain when Alyssa's coffin was lowered into the ground. Alyssa's lashes lowering over her eyes as she'd drifted off to sleep that last day. Bree kneeling in his yard, surrounded by vivid bursts of color, tending to the flowers she'd helped Alyssa plant.

Alyssa... How often she'd been whispering to him over the past six months. But what if it wasn't her? What if she really wasn't okay with the fact that he found himself looking at Bree and realizing he had feelings for her? What if it was just some rationalization his guilty conscience had dreamed up?

Reaching out, he closed a hand over the doorknob, turned it slowly. He pushed it open and sagged against the door frame.

Sunlight drifted in through the windows to fall across the bed in pale splashes of gold. The hospital bed had been removed. Bree must have taken care of that. Their old bed was back where it had always been, neat as a pin. His throat went tight as he made himself walk into the room.

He closed his eyes and took a deep breath, dragging the air into his lungs. Before, the room had always smelled of Alyssa—sexy and female. Now the air had a sterile quality, the faint scent of lemon-scented Pledge lingering in the air and nothing else. On the dresser, he could see her hair brush and a tangle of silver and gold chains thrown onto a silver tray. Just as it had been when he left.

Colby crossed to the dresser and stroked a finger down the tray's edge. It was an antique that she'd found at some garage sale or second-hand store. Alyssa had used to love going to places like that. When she had brought this tray home, it had been all but black with tarnish.

Tugging open the top drawer, he found himself staring at silk and lacy swathes of filmy material that hadn't hidden a damn thing when she wore them. Hooking a finger in something Alyssa had called peacock blue, he lifted it up. It just looked blue to him.

It was a chemise, so damn skimpy she couldn't wear it for anything other than driving him crazy. She'd loved lingerie. He'd loved seeing her in it. Loved buying it for her and wondering when she'd wear it for him. So why in hell couldn't he remember how she looked wearing this?

Something dark and bitter moved through him and he crumpled the filmy bit of nothing in his hand, glaring at his reflection in the mirror. She'd been dead a year and he was already starting to forget how she looked. A year and he was already so damn hot to fuck her best friend, he'd all but stripped her naked in public. So damn ready to do whatever the hell he wanted that he was dreaming up ghosts just to rationalize and make it all okay.

"She wasn't anywhere close to being naked. And I'm not a rationalization, babe."

Colby wheeled around, following the sound of her voice. When he saw Alyssa sitting on the edge of the bed, the bed visible through her, he stumbled back. His butt bumped into the dresser and that was all that stopped him, otherwise he just might have kept backing away. "You aren't real."

Alyssa sighed and tucked a wayward curl behind her ear. "Didn't we already talk about this? I am real. As real as a dead person can be, anyway." Then she winked at him. "I wasn't ever the rational type, so don't try to use rationality to explain me away."

"You can't be real."

She shrugged. "People say that about Bigfoot too, but you believe in him. Why can't you believe in me?"

He scowled at her. She was right. She hadn't ever been the rational type. Not too many people, besides her, could draw a connection between her transparent form and the existence of a cryptid. "I believe he *could* exist. I don't necessarily think he *does* exist."

She gave him a brilliant smile. "Then you could at least give me the benefit of the doubt and believe I could exist."

She glanced down and Colby followed the line of her gaze until he realized she was looking at the blue chemise he still held clutched in his hand. "I went shopping with Bree the day I bought that."

"So what? You went shopping with Bree all the time."

"She picked it out."

He turned and shoved it into the dresser, unsure why he had to get it out of his sight. He lifted his gaze and stared into the mirror. *I'll be damned*, he thought. *Ghosts do cast reflections.* And he could see hers rising from the bed and moving toward him. "And that matters...why? Weren't you trying to convince me the other day that Bree has some secret hang-up on me? Why the hell would she help you pick out lingerie if she had something for me?"

Alyssa shrugged. "Maybe because she was doing what friends do."

She stood beside him now, staring at her reflection with wide, curious eyes. "I haven't been in here since it happened," she whispered. Slowly, she turned and stared around, her gaze lingering on the bed, then moving to the window. "I remember...you lay down next to me, held me. I told you I loved you. You said it back. I wanted to go out to the garden...was going to tell you that after I woke up. But I never did, did I?"

In a rusty, tight voice, he said, "No."

Turning back, she stared down at the jewelry on the tray, lifting a hand as though she'd pick something up, but all she did was let her fingers hover just above the chains. "I can't do anything about you feeling guilty, Colby. I wish I could, but you're the only one who can do something about that. There is nothing for you to feel guilty about. Nothing."

"How can you say that? I'm back here a month and all I can think about is her."

"That's not really true." Alyssa lowered her hand to her side and then faced him. "You're too hung up on feeling guilty for Bree to be everything you think about, or you would have already at least slept with her."

"It shouldn't be like this," he gritted out. "You weren't even gone six months when I started dreaming about her. That isn't right."

Alyssa cocked a brow at him. "Says who?"

And that wasn't something he really had an answer for. She smiled at him, rose up on her toes. A chill caressed his lips as she pressed her mouth to his. He couldn't feel her, not really, just the brush of something cold—there, then gone. "Stop beating yourself up, baby. It really is okay to let me go. And it really is okay to love her."

"I don't..." He wanted to say he didn't love Bree. There was no rhyme or reason to it. He'd known her for as long as he'd known Alyssa and up until a year ago, she'd been his wife's best friend. His friend. Nothing else. Then he had started having bizarre dreams about her. "That doesn't make sense."

She shrugged. "Love never does." Slowly, she backed away and whispered, "You have to decide to let me go. Until you do that, until you really do it, you're going to live with the guilt. And you're going to live with wanting her and not having her. Wanting something you can't have sucks, baby. You know that. So just let me go."

Guilty Needs

* * * * *

Let me go.

Colby stood in the same spot three hours later.

The same spot, but nothing in the room looked the same. Most of the walls were bare. He had boxed up all of Alyssa's clothes, along with her shoes, her jewelry, her books.

Everything.

Empty boxes had been down in the garage, waiting for him.

Now, there was only one thing left.

Lowering his gaze, he stared at the ring on his finger. It didn't come off easily. He still hadn't put on the fifteen pounds he'd lost over the past year, but the ring didn't want to come off. When it did, he started to add it to the boxes piled on the bed, but instead, laid it on the dresser.

He was having the local DAV store pick up Alyssa's clothes and stuff, but he couldn't part with his ring so easily.

With one last, lingering glance, he left the room and slipped outside.

* * * * *

He hadn't known exactly where he planned to go—at least not until he was pulling into her driveway.

He should have though.

He thought about her too often. He could hear her laugh in his sleep, smell the scent of her skin even when she wasn't there and when she smiled, it hit him in the chest like a ton of bricks.

Bree.

Maybe he was falling in love with her...no, screw the maybe. He was pretty sure he already was. But could she love him back?

He didn't know. She was sitting on the front porch when he pulled up, almost as though she'd been waiting for him. With her head leaning back against the plush cushion of the porch swing, she watched him as he climbed out of his car, mounted the steps and crossed to stand before her.

"I forgot to bring your bike back." She shrugged. Her silken skin gleamed gold against the pale green tank-top she wore. Her eyes were carefully blank. "No big deal. I've got the truck. How did you get the car back?"

He glanced over his shoulder and said, "Callie. She came by to clean and I asked her to drop me off."

She was quiet, saying nothing else, just staring at him, no expression on her face. His heart kept skipping beats, dancing around erratically while heat and need sizzled through him. Damn it, he wanted her.

Needed.

But she was so damn quiet, so reserved, and he didn't know if she'd welcome him if he touched her again or jerk away.

Voice ragged, he asked, "Are you mad at me?"

Her lashes lowered briefly over her eyes. She was quiet for a second, long enough to have his stomach going into knots. "No, I'm not mad at you."

"Should I apologize?"

She blinked. "Why?"

"Because if it's something I should be sorry for, then I won't do it again. Should I be sorry?"

Her tongue slid out, slicked across her lips. "No." Her voice was all but soundless. "Nothing to be sorry for."

He crouched down in front of her and gingerly laid his hands on her thighs. She wore a denim skirt that was too damn short for his state of mind and the long, lean expanse of her legs bared all but had him drooling. He stroked down low. What he wanted to do was stroke up. Up under the skirt, to tug her panties down and strip them away. Then hold the skirt out of the way as he pressed his mouth to her and licked her pussy until she came.

That was what he wanted.

But instead of doing that, he murmured, "And what if I want to do it again? And more?"

"Do you?" She stared at him from hooded eyes.

In response, he shifted his left hand higher, pushing it under the hem of her skirt and brushing the tips of his fingers against her heated sex. "Yes," he said, his voice harsh and guttural.

"Why?"

He touched her again, a firmer touch. He could feel the hot silk of her through her panties. "Because I've been thinking about doing it for six months now and it's driving me crazy wondering."

She blinked, her lashes so low over her eyes that all he could see was a thin sliver of gray. Then she arched her hips up, oh-so slightly and rubbed against his fingers. "So is this for the sake of curiosity?"

"No." He hooked an arm around her hips and hauled her to the edge of the swing. "If it was just for the sake of curiosity, I could have fucked you that day before I left—you would have let me. I could see it in your eyes." Then he slanted his mouth against hers and kissed her.

At the same time, he hooked his thumb inside the leg of her panties and drew it away from her sex. As he pushed his tongue into her mouth, he slid two fingers inside her pussy. Hot, molten satin—she was tight, fiery and sweetly wet. He withdrew his fingers, and as he stroked back, he twisted his wrist, screwing his fingers in and out. She moaned into his mouth, her back arching.

She went tight around him—too tight. Each successive touch made her burn hotter around him, had her silken sheath clenching tighter and tighter. Before Colby even realized how close she was, she came, muffling her cry against his mouth and rocking desperately against his hand.

Dragging his mouth away from hers, he swore and shifted. She must have thought he was going to pull away because she cried out and caught his wrist, holding him as she worked herself against his hand.

"Shh...it's okay," he muttered against her trembling mouth. Then he disentangled them, reluctantly withdrawing his fingers. He pulled her off the swing, all too conscious of how exposed they were, but he couldn't have found the strength to pull away if he had to, not even just to take her into the house.

Instead, he settled on the wooden-plank floor, with his back against the high railing. The railing and the hedge between them and the street should—hopefully—block them from view.

He sat with her between his thighs, her back pressed to his chest, her body still trembling, still tight with need.

She whimpered as he stroked his hand down the center of her body. When he cupped her in his hand, she shuddered and a rush of wet heat met him as he parted her flesh and sank his fingers back inside her.

A neat patch of black curls shielded her pussy and through the curls, he could see the swollen, erect bud of her clit. Resting his chin on her shoulder, he stared down at her body, watched the way his hands looked on her as he stroked her clit, as he sank his fingers deep inside her pussy.

Like a fucking fantasy.

That was how it looked.

His mouth watered with the need to push her to the ground and lie between her thighs and lap at her dew-slicked pussy, suck on her clit until she erupted and then crawl up her body and bury his cock inside her.

Instead, he stayed where he was, watching as he teased, stroked and caressed. She whimpered, mewled and moaned his name, rocking against his hand, reaching up and back, twining one arm around his neck.

This time, when he felt the orgasm moving on her, he pressed his thumb to her clit and rubbed. Slow, careful strokes that quickly became frenzied as she bucked against him with some sort of desperate hunger.

She climaxed with a harsh, broken moan before going limp in his arms.

He felt it when the languor faded. Although he was still burning from his own needs, all he wanted to do was sit there and hold her. But she tore away from him, lurched to her feet and stumbled away. Her hands shook as she smoothed her skirt down and her pretty caramel-colored skin was a deep shade of dusky pink.

She wouldn't look at him.

But for some reason, Colby didn't need her to. He got to his feet and moved to stand behind her, wrapping his arms around her when she would have shrugged him away. Her body was tense in his arms, stiff and unyielding. In that moment, though, she could have surrounded herself with slobbering pit bulls and he wouldn't have been fooled.

She did want him.

A hell of a lot.

Him. Maybe even as intensely as he wanted her.

"Have dinner with me."

She glanced up over her shoulder at him and then away. "Why?"

"Because it seems like I ought to buy you a meal before I talk you out of your clothes?" he teased, trying to keep it light.

"Why do you want to talk me out of anything?"

He let go of her arms, but before she could slip away, he snagged her waist, working one arm around her and holding her steady as he rocked his cock against the soft, plump curve of her ass. "Because I can't stop thinking about you. And because I want to see you smiling at me when I wake up in the morning." He stroked his other hand up her side and cupped her breast. "Have dinner with me."

"And then what? A quick fuck and then we go back to being friends?"

He whirled her around in his arms and caught her face in his hands. "It won't be quick…well, maybe the first time. But not the second. Not the third. And you and I both know we've gone past being just friends. I don't know how exactly that happened, but it has happened. The question is — where do we go from here?" He pressed his mouth to hers but didn't kiss her. He whispered, "I spent the last year running. I'm tired of it. Aren't you?"

She sighed shakily. "Colby, you sure this is a good idea?"

With a soft laugh, he murmured, "Hell if I know. I just know it feels right. So what's your answer?"

She licked her lips. He felt the brush of her tongue against his own mouth and growled, wanting to suck it in and bite down — just a little — until he felt her shudder against him. Instead, he lifted his head and stared down at her. "Well?"

Her nod was hesitant. Her voice soft. "Dinner."

But her eyes were hotter than molten steel and Colby knew he could get lost in them — would get lost in them — if he wasn't careful.

Slowly, he let her go. Catching her hand, he lifted it to his lips and brushed a kiss to the back of it. "Eight o'clock."

"Eight."

He took another step back and then made himself turn around before he grabbed her again. He managed to get exactly five feet away before he turned back, took two long strides and reached for her, cupping her face in his hands and kissing her until she moaned into his mouth. He sucked gently, drawing her tongue to him and as she slid it along his lower lip, then inside his mouth. Colby bit — gently. Softly.

Guilty Needs

Before he could do anything else, he let her go, turned on his heel and stalked away from her.

The next three hours were going to take entirely too long.

Chapter Seven

She looked beautiful in the candlelight, Colby decided.

Beautiful. Shy. Nervous. When she caught him looking at her, she'd bite her lip and look away as though she didn't know what to say. It wasn't something he was used to from her, but hell, he hadn't exactly pictured the two of them in a date situation, or at least not for a good fifteen years. And a date situation for a fifteen-year-old boy was a hell of a lot different than a date situation for a thirty-year-old man.

"I never told you that I had a crush on you in high school, did I?" he asked, out of the blue. The second it left his mouth, he wondered why the hell he'd brought that up but he couldn't exactly regret it, either. Not once he caught sight of the look on her face.

Her eyes went wide, her jaw dropped open and then she snapped it closed. "You did not."

Leaning back, he shrugged and said, "Yeah, I did. But you were more interested in basketball practice and doing whatever you used to do with Alyssa. You never noticed me."

Something odd moved through her eyes and she smiled sadly. "I noticed you. Alyssa just noticed you first."

He wanted to ask her what she meant by that, but then the waiter appeared. They ordered, both of them going for the New York strip. Bree ordered a rum and coke, but he stuck with ice water. Forcing a smile, he said, "I did a little too much drinking after I took off. Figure it's better just to not go there again."

She glanced toward the waiter. "Maybe I..."

"Don't worry about it. Doesn't bother me or anything. And I'm not exactly an alcoholic looking to fall off the wagon. I just hit it harder than I should have, and when I realized it, I made myself stop." Okay, truth doctored a little there. He hadn't realized it. That was when Alyssa had first starting talking to him, her voice whispering to him in the night, and he'd been convinced it was because he was so damn drunk he was imagining it, or because he losing his grip on reality.

Neither appealed. If he was looking insanity straight the eye, he couldn't do much about it but he could do something about the drinking. That was exactly what he had done—emptied out every last bit of alcohol he had stashed in the one-room efficiency apartment he rented by the week and he hadn't had a drop since.

The fucked-up dreams about Bree had started a few weeks before that and because of them, he'd been drinking even more than normal. Part of him had hoped that, when he quit the drinking, the dreams and the whisper of Alyssa's voice would stop. Didn't happen.

"You look serious."

He glanced up, pulled out of his retrospection and found Bree eyeing him with carefully guarded eyes. "Just thinking."

He shrugged his brooding thoughts away, studying her from across the table. It was in that moment that he realized she almost always looked guarded—at least when he was around. If he happened upon her and caught her by surprise, it wasn't there. But as soon as she saw him, the walls went up. He drummed his fingers on his thigh under the table and decided he didn't like it. The few times he hadn't seen it had been the day of the funeral, the other day when he'd kissed her and today on her porch.

Unable to stop it, a grin spread across his face, or it might have been more of a leer—hell if he knew. When she saw it, she flushed, her cheeks turning a dusky shade of pink as she squirmed in the seat. "What?" she asked defensively.

"Just thinking—different sort of thoughts this time." His gaze dropped, following the rosy blush down to her neckline where the deep vee of her blouse blocked his view. Her nipples were hard.

Her blush deepened as she crossed her arms over her chest. "Would you stop?" she asked, exasperated.

"I'm not doing anything," he said, though he knew it wasn't exactly true. He made her nervous.

Bree. Of all the women he knew, she was the last one he would have expected to be nervous around him. Was it a new thing? Or just something she'd hidden?

The waiter appeared once again, quiet and fast, placed a rum-and-coke in front of Bree, then disappeared as quietly as he'd arrived. She grabbed it, took one large gulp, then another. From under her lashes, she watched him.

"What about you?"

She frowned at him. "What do you mean, what about me?"

He shrugged restlessly. "Who did you have some secret crush on in high school? Basketball player? Somebody on the football team?"

She took another sip from her drink and then set it on the table before answering. "High school was fifteen years ago. I barely remember half the kids in my homeroom class."

"You telling me you don't remember your biggest crush in high school?"

Rolling her eyes, she said, "What does it matter? It was high school."

"Just making conversation. I don't really remember ever seeing you hang out with a particular guy." And he would have noticed, at least if it happened during their freshman year or even halfway through their sophomore year. Probably even beyond, because even though he stopped thinking about her like that, she had been his girl's best friend. Most teens did double dates from time to time, but Bree hadn't. Hell, come to think about it, he really couldn't think of a single guy throughout high school that she'd really spoken to.

In college, she'd dated some. He could remember those guys. One had been a jackass and she'd dumped him after two dates. One had lasted a few months. During their senior year, the guy she had dated had actually lasted throughout the year. That one had seemed serious but then the guy had died.

"You don't date much."

It wasn't a question and she didn't treat it as one. A wry smile curled her lips and she lifted one shoulder carelessly. "I'm picky."

"Picky about what?"

"The guys I date."

"What are you so picky about?" Bracing his elbows on the table, he leaned forward. What made a woman so picky that she went on less than two or three dates a year? He knew she got asked out a lot—or at least it seemed a regular occurrence, from what he'd seen. No surprise. She was flat-out sexy, she was funny in a quiet, understated way and she was one of the kindest people he'd ever known.

"Maybe I just haven't found what I'm looking for yet."

"What are you looking for?"

She rolled her eyes. "Geez, Colby, what is this? Twenty questions? If a guy asks me out and I'm interested, I'll go out with him. I'm usually just not interested."

"You're here with me."

Her dark-gray eyes narrowed and she said acerbically, "So apparently, I'm not picky enough. I hadn't realized I was going to get the Spanish Inquisition."

He slid his hand across the table and took hers. Lacing their fingers together, he whispered, "If we're doing an inquisition, does that mean I can get you on the rack later?"

Her eyes widened. A startled laugh escaped her and she clapped her free hand over her mouth, muffling the sound. "I don't do racks on the first date."

He was flirting with her. Okay, Bree wasn't an idiot, but it took her a little while to actually realize the truth. Colby was actually flirting with her. *Why the hell is that such a shock? He had his hand in your panties and his tongue halfway down your throat a couple of hours ago. He more or less said he wanted to sleep with you. Why shouldn't he flirt?*

Still—it was weird. Seriously weird.

And unsettling as hell. Not just because it felt like some bizarre fantasy come to life either. *You and I both know we've gone past being just friends.* Actually, she hadn't let herself think along those lines, even after he'd kissed her outside the winery. She just wasn't ready to let herself think about that, because Bree was a linear type of thinker. If she knew one thing was coming, she started to plan for what happened after.

Here, the "after" that seemed most likely was that Colby wasn't seriously interested in her and once he got whatever this was out of his system, she'd go back to being a friend— probably not even that.

Definitely not something she was equipped for.

By the time the waiter brought the check, she felt as though she was going to splinter into a thousand pieces from the pressure. Trying to keep it light, trying not to let him see how he affected her, trying not to read too much into his casual, sexy flirtation.

The ride home was a little easier—not having to sit across from him, staring at the perfect face with his sexy mouth and those amber eyes, having to sit still while he looked at her with such heat that she could almost feel it stroking over her skin. He pulled into her driveway and she bent to get her purse from the floor. He was already halfway around the car and when she opened her door, he was there with his hand outstretched.

Tucking her hand into his arm, he guided her around the side of the house, instead of in. Bree lived in the house where she'd grown up, under the care of her aunt. When her aunt moved to Florida a few years after Bree graduated from college, she had bought the house and spent the past eight years working on it.

The backyard looked like something straight out of *Extreme Home Makeover*—an outdoor kitchen complete with a stone firepit, a small swimming pool, water gardens, every last inch of ground perfectly landscaped. It was her pride and joy and normally, she loved being out here.

But for some reason, tonight, here in the darkness with Colby, it was unsettling, to say the least.

The neighborhood where she lived was an older one and the lots were huge. Tall privacy fences separated the yards and the vining plants that she had growing along the perimeter inside her yard only added to the sense of seclusion. He unlatched the gate and guided her inside with his hand resting low on her back.

"I think, if you want to tell me to go home, now's going to be a good time."

She glanced up at him. It was a full moon and the silvery light shown down on him, highlighting the planes and hollows of his face, revealing the heat in his eyes—a heat he'd made little attempt to disguise during the night. Her head was spinning. She could barely keep up with the changes in him, going from quiet, brooding widower to sexy, flirtatious charmer. None of it made sense and if she was smart, she'd tell him it was best to call it a night.

But Bree couldn't say it.

Fifteen years of fantasy stood next to her and even if she ended up getting her heart broken, at least she'd have something, right?

"You know, you're confusing the hell out of me," she said, keeping her tone light. Slipping her arm away from his, she reached down and unbuckled her shoes. Stepping out of them, she carried them over to the porch and laid them down, along with her purse. Then she turned to face him, her arms hanging loose at her sides, her heart pounding with anticipation and nerves.

"How?"

Bree shook her head. "You just are. Five weeks ago, I had no idea where you were, if you were ever going to come home. Then you're here, but you're not...not quite you. Grief is a bitch, I know. It does weird things to people..."

Her voice trailed off and she licked her lips. She lifted a hand futilely, as though she could pull the words from the air. But words were his thing. Not hers. "Then all of a sudden, you're flirting with me, teasing me. You kiss me, tell me you want to sleep with me."

She eyed him nervously. He stood mostly in shadow now, the moon at his back, throwing his features into darkness. She could make out the hungry glitter of his eyes but not much more than that. "So what is this? You trying yourself out on training wheels or something before you rejoin the land of the living?"

He snorted. "Shit, you don't think much of me, do you, Bree?"

"Actually, I think the world of you." *You have absolutely no idea just how much I think of you. If you knew just how much I think of you, you'd probably take off running.* "I just..." her voice trailed off and she sighed. "I don't know what you want."

He didn't say anything right away, but she could all but hear him laying out his thoughts. Sometimes, it seemed this man spent way too much time thinking, and when he spent a lot of time thinking, she had to wonder what that meant for her. He paced toward her, not speaking until he was close, so close she could feel the heat of his body. "I want you."

"But for what? For a night? For a few nights? You just need to take the edge off? What? I like knowing what I'm getting into and I can't tell with you."

He cupped a hand over the back of her neck, drawing her close until he could press his brow to hers. "I've been dreaming of you nearly every damn night for the past six months. I wake up half sick with guilt and feeling like the lowest life form in existence because of those dreams. Alyssa's only been gone a year but I've spent half of that year obsessed with her best friend. Whatever is going on inside me isn't something that's going to go away after one night, two nights—probably not even if we spent the next six months in bed." He brushed his lips over hers.

If he hadn't been standing so close she could lean against him, her quivering legs just might have given way beneath her. But then he stepped away and she wobbled, automatically throwing out a hand and grabbing onto him. He covered her hand with his and with his other, he cupped her cheek. "But if this isn't something you want, you better tell me now."

He stroked his thumb over her lip and gazed down at her.

It was her call.

Bree knew if she told him to leave, he'd do just that. In all likelihood, whatever chance it was that lay before her would be gone. Colby wouldn't do this again. If she pushed him away, she knew she'd never have this chance again.

Not that pushing him away was even a possibility. For her, it never had been. The minute he made it clear that he wanted her, she'd been his. All the words, all her worries and doubts and fears, none of it made any difference. Words. She closed her eyes, wished she could find the words to tell him what was inside her, but they weren't there.

Words. They were his thing. Not hers.

But she didn't need words.

Slowly, she stepped back. His hand fell away and as she watched, his gaze became shuttered, locking her completely out. But, as she reached for the placket of buttons running down the front of her dress, he hissed out a breath. She didn't look at him.

Bree was pretty sure that if she looked at him, she'd freeze. She'd panic. Worse—she'd throw herself at him and ask if he loved her, even a little. She might not even care if he lied. At least not right away.

So instead of looking at him, she kept her lashes low as she worked the dress off. It was a halter style, a complicated thing that buttoned up almost like a man's dress shirt, with a collar and a vee neckline, but it left her shoulders and back bare. It fit close, which meant that even after she unbuttoned it all the way down, she had to shimmy her way out of it. Letting it fall to her feet in a puddle, she stepped out of it.

An attack of nerves seized her, though, and she couldn't finish stripping out of her clothes while standing in front of him. She felt the burn of his gaze following her as she started toward the pool. She undid her strapless bra and dropped it by the pool's edge. The lights in the pool were kept on a timer and in the darkness of the night, the water gleamed a vibrant, jewel-like shade of turquoise. It reflected light off her body as she hooked her thumbs in her panties and pushed them down.

She heard him coming up behind her as she dove into the water and swam along the bottom of the pool until she reached the far edge. She surfaced, rested a hand on the edge and turned her head toward him. He still stood at the other side of the pool. Shoving off the wall, she stroked toward him in a lazy crawl. Her heart leapt as he stripped away his shirt, letting it fall to the stone walkway bordering the pool. After he kicked his shoes off, he crouched down beside the pool and hooked a hand over the back of her neck, drawing her up.

She braced her hands on the lip of the pool and shoved upward, meeting his mouth as he dipped his head and snaking one arm around his shoulders. He traced the edge of her lips with his tongue before pushing inside. She shuddered. Already the need was threatening to spiral out of control. Bree wasn't quite so ready to give into it. Bracing one foot against the pool wall, she shoved.

He tumbled into the water with her, but if she thought that would buy her some breathing room, she'd thought wrong. He kept his arms wrapped around her and took her to the bottom, keeping their mouths fused until the need to breathe drove them to the surface. He swam upward, keeping her body pressed to his. Catching hold of the ladder, he kept them afloat, pressed his brow to hers. "That was mean. You do realize I still have my pants on, don't you?"

She smiled against his lips and slid one hand down his chest. "Oops." It took some fumbling and some patience to strip him out of the wet black trousers. He caught them before they could sink to the bottom and tossed the sodden material onto the walkway.

Sliding her palms into the waistband of the boxer briefs he wore, she brushed the tips of her fingers over the head of his cock. His rigid flesh jerked under her touch and a harsh breath hissed out from between his teeth. "Damn it, Bree."

She grinned as she closed her hand around his cock and stroked. One slow stroke down, one slow stroke up. The cool kiss of water couldn't hide the fiery heat of his penis. The skin stretched over his cock was silken smooth, and underneath, rigid, so damn hard. She realized she was clenching her knees together as her sex throbbed.

She milked him with her hand, staring at his face, lost in the rapture she glimpsed on his features. His head was tilted back, eyes narrowed down to slits, teeth clenched in a hungry grimace. He started to move, rocking forward to meet her hand—quicker, harder.

Then abruptly, he stopped, pulled her hand away and caught her wrist when she would have reached for him again. He kissed her—deep, hard—thrusting his tongue past her lips, devouring her, as though he'd swallow her whole.

He tore his mouth away from hers to blaze a hot, stinging line of kisses up to her ear. "Gimme a break, Bree. Slow it down or this is going to be over before we get to the fun stuff."

Tilting her head to the side, she shivered as he raked his teeth down her neck. "This isn't the fun stuff?"

"Maybe a little fun." He stroked one hand down her side, reaching between them to circle the tip of his finger around the entrance to her pussy. "But the real fun starts here. I want to taste you. I want to bury my dick inside this hot, wet pussy and fuck you until neither of us can handle any more."

Bree whimpered. Dazed, she arched against him and said, "I already can't handle any more. Colby…"

He laughed. "Slow down, beautiful. I haven't waited this long to rush it." His mouth roamed restlessly over her neck and shoulder as, between her thighs, he touched, teased and stroked. Colby dipped his fingers into her aching pussy, while rotating his thumb around her clit, keeping his touch teasingly light.

"Damn it, Colby."

He laughed and looped an arm around her waist. "Take a breath."

The water closed back over them, drifting along her body in a silken, cool caress as he propelled them along the floor until they reached the shallow end. There, he pressed her back against the wall. Just as he pressed against her though, his eyes flashed and he swore. "Damn it. I need my pants."

"No."

It was sheer insanity that drove her—the only explanation—as she twined her legs around his hips before he could pull away. "I'm on the Pill—and I'm clean. I haven't been with…" her voice trailed off as she tried to think how long. Too long. Finishing with a lame shrug, she said, "I'm clean."

Bad move, Colby thought as she rocked against him. *Very, very bad move.*

But he didn't pull away.

He *couldn't* pull away. Her long arms and legs twined around him, but even if she hadn't held him so tightly, he couldn't have pulled away.

He needed her—needed to feel her skin to skin, needed to lose himself inside her. Covering her mouth with his, he shifted the angle of his hips and let her impale herself on his cock.

Her pussy was wet and hot, so damn tight, and before she had taken half his length, she tensed up on him, arching backward. All that did was drive her farther down on his length.

A pained cry escaped her and she twisted, arching and rocking against him. Tension tightly held her body and Colby knew that even as sweet as it felt for him, those clenching, reluctant tissues fighting his intrusion, made it painful her.

Sliding a hand up her thigh, he cupped her hip and whispered, "Relax."

She sighed into his mouth—a shaky, desperate little sound. He caught that sound and then trailed his tongue along her lips, skimmed his hand up her back and fisted his free hand in the short strands of her hair, tugged her head to the side and pressed a kiss to her throat. "Fuck, you're hot, Bree. So damn tight..."

She shivered.

Against his lips, he felt her pulse skip a beat or two. Smiling against her skin, he whispered, "Sweet...hot...wet..."

She whimpered and arched against him, her tight nipples stabbing into his chest.

Bree liked dirty talk.

"You want to know how good you feel?" he asked. Bit by bit, her body eased. Just a little. Until he could sink another inch, then another, into her pussy until she'd taken all of him. "You feel like heaven, like hot, wet, silky heaven."

"Colby..." she whispered, her voice a soft, broken moan.

Working his hand between their bodies, he stroked his thumb around her clit and her hoarse whisper erupted into a harsh sob as he stroked her.

"Fuck, Bree..." he groaned as she climaxed around him, the silken walls of her sheath clenching his cock. He gritted his teeth against the urge to follow her as she whimpered and shuddered her way through orgasm.

Even as her climax passed, she continued to move against him. She was so damn perfect, her pussy gloving him, tight and sweet, clutching at his cock as he withdrew—greedy, demanding. All he wanted to do was give her every last thing she desired...and more.

He needed more—had to have it—but the buoyancy of the water kept him from taking her as deep, as hard as he needed. Growling against her mouth, he pulled away from her only long enough to climb from the pool and then snag her wrist, pulling her along behind him. Water dripped from their bodies as he tumbled her to the wooden chaise by the pool and mounted her, spreading her legs wide and pushing deep. Bracing his elbows next to her, he hooked his arms under her shoulders, twined his hands in her hair and kissed her.

Bree cried out, the sound smothered against his lips. Her short, neatly trimmed nails raked down his back, leaving fiery trails of sensation along the path her hands had taken.

The cool night air danced along his damp body, but for all he knew, they could have been surrounded by a lake of flame, he was so damn hot.

Hotter than hell, and burning even hotter as she moved underneath him, her snug pussy clenching down around him, milking him, drawing him deeper, deeper.

Warning chills danced along his spine. Between his legs, his balls drew tight against him. Tearing his mouth away from hers, he buried his face against her neck. Not yet...

Self-preservation had him slowing down the rhythm of his thrusts. Bree cupped her hands over his hips and tried to draw him closer but he held back. Slow, easy thrust in—slow, easy withdrawal—still, her silk-drenched pussy was fist-tight around him, her scent flooded his head and her soft, hoarse moans were the most erotic sounds he'd ever heard in his life. Control was hard-won, bit by bit, degree by degree and every time she wiggled against him, every time her nails dug into his hips in demand, that hard-won control threatened to shatter.

Six fucking months of dreams weren't going to end in under two minutes, though. Shoving upward, he balanced on his haunches while he hooked his elbows under her knees. Then he covered her again, using his weight to keep her from moving under him as he fucked her.

That sweet, snug pussy convulsed around him as Bree snarled in frustration. Her body tensed as she fought to set the rhythm.

"Be still," Colby muttered, nipping her ear.

"Damn it, Colby—"

He nuzzled her neck. "I haven't spent the last six months dreaming about this just so you can have me coming before I barely even have a chance to start. Be still."

"Six months…" She stretched her arms overhead, her hands scrambling for something to hold on to. All she could find was the wooden chaise they lay on. Gripping it in her hands, she managed, just barely, to get enough leverage to grind her pelvis against his.

She moaned even as he swore, her lashes fluttering low over her eyes. He felt it coming on her, as easy as that, just the friction of his body rubbing against her clit.

She gloved him so tightly, but as she started to come, her pussy squeezed down around his dick in excruciating pleasure-pain.

He wasn't going to be able to hold out this time. He tried, gritting his teeth, dropping his body down on hers and using his weight to pin her in place, but nothing he did could stop the rhythmic, milking caresses rippling along his cock.

Nothing could cool the fire building in his balls, racing up his spine and exploding through him. "Witch," he growled, groaning low in his throat as climax slammed into them. It danced and sizzled through his veins—liquid electricity that started in his fingers, his toes, hurtling inward until it converged in his balls before exploding outward.

He had to see her—needed to see her eyes. "Look at me," he rasped, letting go of her legs. "Look at me..." he laid a hand on her neck, rested his thumb against her lips. Her lashes lifted slowly. She opened her mouth, circled his thumb with her tongue before drawing it inside. She sucked on him as he rode her and the feel of it—her hot mouth drawing on his flesh—had another climax rise up and slam into him before the first one had even ended.

With a hoarse cry, he arched against her, lost in her. Dimly, he felt her body shuddering, shaking, moving in rhythm with his as she came.

And his name.

As he collapsed, to rest with his head pillowed between her breasts, she whispered his name.

Bree had no idea how long they lay there.

It could have been minutes.

It could have been hours.

She might have drifted off for a few minutes, she didn't know. Nothing seemed real, yet it had that vivid, surreal quality of dreams, the kind that lingered with you for hours after waking. It wasn't until he stirred in her arms that her brain actually kicked in and she realized what was going on.

It had all really happened. This wasn't just some midnight fantasy that would shatter around her the minute she opened her eyes. Her body cried out at the loss of his heat as he braced his elbows on the ground and pushed up, staring at her face with unreadable eyes.

The practical bitch trapped inside Bree commented snidely, *Here comes the now-what. You wanted to know. Here's the answer. He's going to stand up, get dressed and walk away.*

Well, one out of three. He did stand up. But he didn't get dressed or walk away. What he did was take her hand and draw her to her feet and guide her to the house. Without speaking, he snagged her purse from the ground and dug out her keys. She wrapped her arms around her body, shivering as the cool summer night air began to penetrate the lax, lazy languor that wrapped around her.

Inside the house wasn't much better. Her nipples were so tight from the cool air, they ached and she shivered uncontrollably until he stopped mid-step and scooped her up in his arms. She squealed, startled, and immediately felt like an idiot. Smacking at his shoulders, she squirmed. "Put me down, Colby. I'm too heavy."

He nuzzled her neck and then smiled down at her, his eyes heavy-lidded. "You don't feel too heavy to me." The tips of his fingers touched the outer curve of her right breast and he stroked her lightly. "You feel perfect."

Perfect? She snorted. She stood five inches taller than Alyssa had and probably weighed a good fifty pounds more. *Stop. Stop thinking about her.* She tensed in his arms, unable to banish the overwhelming sense of self-consciousness that washed over her.

"Where did you go?" he asked as he carried her into her room and laid her on the bed.

She might have tried to roll away from him, but he settled down next to her, bracing an arm on her opposite side. Trapped, she stared up at him in the dark room. At least it was dark in there. She always kept her curtains closed so the brilliant silvery light of the full moon couldn't shine through. The darkness made it easier to deal with him.

What could she say? *I keep thinking about Alyssa and I come up short every damn time.* Hell, now that would put a damper on things. Instead, she hedged, looking away from him as she mumbled, "I'm nowhere near perfect, Colby."

He left the bed. Tracking his shadowed body, she watched as he made his way back to the door. As he flicked the light on, she flinched, automatically shielding her eyes. Squinting at him, she watched as he moved to the foot of the bed. He wrapped his fingers around her ankles, firmly, gently urging her to open her thighs. Then he settled on his knees between her widespread legs and laid the flats of his palms on the outer curve of her calves. His eyes roamed over her, starting at her legs, moving upward.

As he stared at her sex, blood rushed to her cheeks but she couldn't tell if she was more turned-on or embarrassed. She was already wet—wet from herself, wet from him—but under that hot, intense stare, she felt a rush of heat escape her. She was on fire. Blazing. Dying from the heat.

Then he licked his lips and crouched down, pressing his mouth against her and she mewled, bucking upward. He stroked his tongue down her slit, opening her.

Bree keened out his name and reached down, fisting her hands in his hair. He settled his body between her thighs. She brought her knees up, trying to decide if she wanted to squirm away or tug on his head until he put his mouth on her and put her out of her misery.

Colby seemed to know what she was debating, because he caught her hips in his hands and held her still. He flicked a glance at her and then kissed her—a full, open-mouthed kiss. He nuzzled her clit, licked it, sucked on the sensitized bud until she was shaking and then he started to fuck his tongue in, out...slowly...lazily.

He stroked her with his tongue, groaned against her pussy, and when she bucked against his mouth, he growled—a demanding, greedy sound low in his chest. His hands tightened on her ass and lifted her more fully against him. The lazy, teasing strokes became hungry, frenzied, driving her harder and harder, as though he was trying to devour her. He didn't stop until he'd driven her to climax and then climbed up her body and wedged his hips between her thighs.

Dazed, she watched as he flicked his hair out of his eyes, their dark golden-amber color burning into her. "Perfect," he muttered. He reached between them, wrapping his fingers around his cock and then guiding his length into her.

She took him easier this time but he still moved too damn slow, feeding her one slow inch at a time, as though driving her crazy topped his list of things to do. "Colby…"

"Bree…" he mimicked, smiling down at her. "You're so impatient."

"And you're cruel." Reaching up, she twined her fingers around his neck, bringing his mouth to hers. "Quit teasing me. You have no idea—" she broke off, flushing as she realized what she'd almost said. What she'd almost told him. She covered by kissing him, twining her tongue with his, pulling back to nip his lip.

"Cruel?" he asked when she broke away to gasp for air. "I go down on you and lick you until you scream my name, but I'm cruel?"

Catching her wrists, he stretched her arms over her head, pinning her wrists with one hand. Trailing the fingertips of his free hand along her side, he reached between them and stroked her clit. "Now if I did this until you were just a breath away from coming, that might be cruel."

He strummed her with his fingers, playing her body like a master. And then he did just what he'd threatened, working her until climax was just a whisper away and then he stopped, bringing his fingers to his mouth and licking them clean. "Now that's being cruel."

If she could have reached him, she would have bitten him. She wrapped her legs around his hips, locking her heels just above his butt. "Don't tease me."

"What do you want me to do?"

Her lashes fluttered. What *did* she want him to do? *Oh, baby, don't go there. Don't ask me a question like that.* How could she possibly answer him without exposing herself? Without making a fool of herself or putting him on the spot? "I want you."

"Want me to what?" Disentangling her legs from his hips, he reached between her thighs again, stroked her, quickly, lightly, and then pulled back before she could work herself against his hand. "Want me to make you come? Want me to fuck you…or should I keep being cruel?"

Lowering her lashes, she stared at him through them. Her voice shook as she said, "Fuck me. Please, Colby…I need you to fuck me." *I need you to love me!* But she wasn't going to ask for things she couldn't have.

But even she heard the desperate plea in her voice, something that went deeper than a need for sex — even a need as visceral and primal as this. Something flared in his eyes. Twin flags of color rode high on his cheeks and he hissed a breath between his teeth. He cupped her cheek in his hand. She could feel the wetness from her body on his fingers, smell the combined scents of their previous orgasms on him. "I'll take care of you, Bree," he muttered, crushing his mouth to hers.

He slammed into her full-force, so hard, driving deep — so deep that she knew she'd feel the sweet ache of it come morning. Her body shuddered from the force of his thrusts. She felt bruised inside, overwhelmed outside. She couldn't even scream because his lips were there, catching each and every sound and swallowing it. The thick length of his cock throbbed and jerked inside her pussy. His free hand cupped her ass, his fingers digging into the crevice between her buttocks.

She jerked against his grasp, wanting to touch him, but he didn't let her go. He rode her hard and even when she stiffened, climaxed around him and wailed into his mouth, he didn't stop. He pounded away at her and when she would have sagged, replete and fulfilled, he growled against her mouth and demanded, "Again, damn it. Come again."

He let go of her hands, pulled away and flipped her onto her belly. She started to push upward but he caught her wrists and pinned them to the bed beside her head. Wedging his knees between her thighs, he opened her more fully and covered her body with his, crushing her into the mattress. He couldn't take her as deeply, not with her lying flat on her belly, legs trapped by his. Still, there was something almost painfully erotic about it, the way he fucked her from behind, his cock digging into her sex — hard as iron, hot as molten steel — her wrists braceleted by one of his hands.

The thick stalk of his cock jerked, throbbed inside her and she whimpered, flexing her muscles around him instinctively, trying to hold him inside even as he withdrew.

"Now who's being cruel?" he muttered, raking his teeth along her shoulder. "Perfect. Hot. Sweet. Come. Come for me, Bree."

"I can't..." she whimpered, even as she lifted her ass, pressing against him, seeking more.

He slid a hand down her side and gripped her hip. "Yeah, you can." He let go of her wrists and settled back on his heels, urging her up onto her knees. Then he slid a hand around her, tweaking her clit, rolling it between his thumb and forefinger, tugging, stroking, rubbing...

"Ohhhhhh..." She whimpered and shuddered, rocking back and forth, riding the thick pillar of flesh, rubbing against his hand — back and forth, back...forth... She straightened, settling back against his body, his chest pressed against her back.

He wrapped his forearm around her waist, steadying her body as she rode him. With his other hand, he continued to stroke her clit, teasing the swollen bud. Every touch was a mix of pleasure and pain, heaven and hell.

"Come." He growled it, that sexy, harsh sound that rumbled out from deep inside his chest and shuddered over her like a velvet caress.

She did, on a low, harsh moan, exploding, everything inside her flying apart. *She* was flying. Soaring off someplace just this side of paradise and if he hadn't held her so close, cradled her so tightly, she just might have gotten so lost in the pleasure, she would never have returned from it.

Distantly, she felt the jerk and throb of his cock as he emptied himself deep inside, flooding her with the hot, wet splash of semen. He whispered her name, his voice a mix of pride and awe.

The whisper came to her through a clouded haze of need and exhaustion, following her into dreams.

* * * * *

She came awake slowly, her body wrapped in heat. An unconscious smile curled her lips as she stretched, arching her back as the vivid dream from last night began to dance through her brain.

"Morning."

Her mouth went dry. Slowly, she pushed up onto her elbow and looked downward. There was an arm wrapped around her waist. Muscled, lightly dusted dark hair. Slightly boney wrist, long-fingered hands... She knew those hands.

Oh, damn do I know those hands. They are the most perfect, most beautiful hands in the world.

Squinting, she sat up and looked down at Colby. His lids were still closed, a smile playing at the corners of his lips but he most definitely was there.

Nonchalantly, she slid her hand under the sheet and pinched her thigh. Hard. The sharp pain didn't make her wake up, which meant only one thing, as far as she could tell. This wasn't a dream.

Last night hadn't been a dream.

"Good morning."

He rolled over onto his back and reached for her, pulling her with him so that she ended up sprawled across him. His lashes lifted and she found herself staring into sleepy, sexy eyes. This was new territory for her. The last time she'd spent a night with a guy had been in college.

Wayne had been the only man she'd met who had ever been able to make her think about somebody besides Colby. She'd loved him. It hadn't been the all-consuming need she had for Colby, but she'd loved him. His sudden death in a car crash had shaken her to the core.

The few times she'd spent the night with him in college, it had always been at his small apartment just off campus. Never once had she had a guy spent the night with her, slept all night in her bed.

Hell, she'd never let a guy *in* her bed.

So this was definitely unchartered territory.

She licked her lips and tried a smile. It wobbled a little, but Colby didn't seem to notice. He stroked a hand up her back and curved it over the nape of her neck, drawing her face toward his.

He kissed her—a lazy, sweet kiss that left her tingling all over, from her lips all the way down to the soles of her feet. His other hand rested on the base of her spine, just above her ass. Against her belly, she felt the rigid length of his cock. With a hungry moan, she rocked against him. The hand on her back slid down, cupped her ass and squeezed.

Lifting up, she shifted until she straddled his thighs. Staring at him, she ran her hands down his chest. His skin was shades paler than her own, sleek and leanly muscled. A smattering of black hair across his pecs trailed down in a thin ribbon that arrowed toward his sex. Her mouth went dry as she stared at him.

His cock was thick, ruddy and swollen. As she stared at him, his flesh jerked. Reaching out, she wrapped her fingers around him and stroked.

He really was here. Lying in her bed. He'd spent the whole night with her and right now, he was looking at her as though nobody else in the world existed. She didn't expect that to last. What had brought him to her like this, she didn't know, but she had no illusions that she was going to have a happily-ever-after wrapped up and placed before. She was too practical to waste time deluding herself.

But she had every intention of enjoying it while it lasted.

Lifting her gaze back to his face, she watched as she stroked him up and down, squeezing as she neared the base of his cock and then easing her grip just a bit as she started the upstroke.

The skin stretched over his rigid length was silky soft, almost fragile. Underneath, he was hard as iron and his flesh jerked in her hand as she stroked upward, then back down, from base to tip, over and over. A clear bead of fluid formed on the head of his penis and she caught it with her thumb and rubbed it around. His breath hissed out from between his teeth. His hips moved in rhythm with her hand and she waited until his body went tense under hers and then she lifted up. Staring down into his eyes, she held him steady as she took his cock inside her.

She sank down on him slowly. Her pussy, swollen and sensitive from last night, resisted it at first and she had to work to take all of him. She could feel every damn ridge and line of his cock—the flared head, the vein running down the underside. Every jerk and throb of his penis sent a flutter of pleasure-pain rushing through her.

It was almost too much, the sensations almost too painful. But she couldn't have made herself stop for anything. She needed him—oh, damn did she *need*.

His hands cupped her hips, fingers biting into her flesh. His head ground into the pillow beneath it, his teeth bared in a sexy snarl. "Fuck, Bree..."

Biting her lip, she took him deeper, but pain flared. She tensed against him, her pussy clutching tight, fighting his cock's slow invasion. She started to lift up. His hands clamped down and he drove upward. She cried out as he forced her down on his cock, impaling her. Arching her back, she held still, her body working to accommodate him, torn between the need to move against him and the need to pull away.

"I'm sorry," he whispered hoarsely, staring up at her through slitted eyes. One hand left her hip, his fingers seeking out the stiff bud of her clit. "Damn it, I'm sorry...fuck, Bree, baby, you're killing me...so fucking perfect..."

She hissed, her hips jerking back but there was no escape. His cock throbbed inside her pussy, stretching her. Undeterred, he stroked her clit, keeping his touch light, soft until need overcame the discomfort and she started to move against him. Falling forward, she braced her hands on the bed on either side of his head.

Heat...need...love threatened to swamp her, threatened to drown her. Words she knew she couldn't say to him lodged in her throat, begging for release. In desperation, she slanted her mouth across his, kissing him, letting her body and her mouth do the talking for her.

His hand cradled the back of her head, the other gripped her hip, steadying her as they moved against each other. Her broken moans were muffled against his mouth.

Eventually, blind desire drowned out anything and everything but the pulse of his cock as he shafted her. His mouth moved greedily against hers, as though he were every bit as starved for her as she was for him.

She even let herself believe that. For a little while. Let herself believe it as she rode him to a climax that left her dazed, drained and utterly drunk on bliss.

Chapter Eight

Bree realized she was actually very good at suppressing her practical side.

That nagging, annoying bitch who kept whispering she really needed to talk things over with Colby and figure out exactly where they stood.

Suppressing her in favor of the giddy, lovelorn woman who took over every time Colby showed up on her doorstep, every time he called.

It wasn't quite as easy to shut her up when she was working, or on the rare nights when he wasn't sharing her bed. A few weeks had gone by before it dawned on her that he was at her house more often than he was home. Bit by bit, he seemed to be settling into her life and it felt so natural, felt so right that it just made it that much easier to ignore that nagging, practical bitch who wanted reality to intrude on Bree's fantasy come to life.

What the hell did it matter that she didn't know where she stood with him?

In that minute, it didn't seem to matter at all. She sat at her breakfast bar, drinking steaming hot coffee and watching as he whipped up a couple of ham-and-cheese omelets. Her belly rumbled demandingly as the tantalizing aroma filled the air. By the time he slid one onto a plate and set it in front of her, Bree was all but drooling.

Regular sex sure as hell did a number on the appetite, she'd discovered. So much so that she had decided the other day that she was going to have to start running on a more regular basis and watch what she ate. Food was little more than a necessity for her, or so she'd thought, but between the

Guilty Needs

way Colby moved in the bedroom and the way he moved in the kitchen, she'd discovered there was a lot more pleasure to a meal than she'd realized. Eating alone was depressing as hell. But put this man into the equation and meals took on a different slant.

"How busy is your schedule today?" he asked, settling across from her with his plate full of food.

He'd put on a little bit of the weight he'd lost over the past eighteen months. His cheeks no longer had that hollow look. It was probably her imagination, but he seemed pretty damn happy.

Focusing on the question, she shrugged and said, "Pretty light. Two clients this morning, one this afternoon, but I'll probably head out early from that one. Pretty standard stuff and my guys can handle it without me." She cut into her omelet and popped a bite into her mouth. The cheese ended up burning her tongue but it was so damn good that she didn't care and cut off another bite, eating it just as quickly. "I've got a pretty busy schedule for the next month or so, though. Starting Monday. Our bid was accepted for the new subdivision going up on the hill and they're about ready for us to get started on the grounds."

This job was going to hopefully give her the money she needed to expand her business a little. She needed more room, an office that wasn't run out of her garage, and more men. If things went well over the next month or so, she'd have it. She even had her eye on a place and had been juggling figures in her head to make sure she could afford it. Right now, if she cleaned out her savings and ate mac and cheese for a few months, she could do it, but she'd have nothing left over. Bree didn't like taking those sorts of risks, so when her bid was accepted, she'd been ecstatic. She could buy the property, hire two new guys and maybe even have the money for some new equipment if she was careful.

Taking a sip of her coffee, she studied him from across the table and asked, "What about you?"

He grimaced. "I finished up that book. Got to put a proposal together and shoot it off to Angela. Assuming she hasn't forgotten who I am."

Bree grinned at him. "I'm pretty sure she hasn't forgotten your name yet."

"I disappeared for more than a year. I'm probably not ranking high on her list of favorite authors." He shrugged and took another bite of his omelet, but she could tell he was worried.

That was good, though. At least, she thought it was. He'd lost interest in his career once it had become clear that Alyssa wasn't going to beat the cancer. Seeing him worrying about it was a positive sign in Bree's mind.

"I don't know how the writer/agent deal works but if she had problems with you taking some time away, wouldn't she have to let you know she was going to…I dunno… Can she fire you?"

Colby grinned at her. "No, but she could drop me from her list of authors. And I don't really see her doing that because of this but that doesn't mean she's going to be all that thrilled with me either."

"Colby, your wife died. Only a heartless bitch wouldn't understand that you might need some time to deal."

As soon as she said it, she wished she could yank it back. She'd been so fucking careful not to put Alyssa between them like that and then she had to go and shove her foot in her mouth. Hell, not just her foot—halfway past her ankle, probably.

His smile faded and he laid the fork down, bracing his elbows on the table. "I know she'll understand but that doesn't mean I'm necessarily going to get my career back on track. Authors disappear all the time. All it takes is not getting a book out often enough."

Bree slid off the stool and went around to stand behind him. Draping her arms over his shoulders, she pressed her cheek to his. "Readers haven't forgotten about you, Colby. They want more from you. Your agent's a smart lady. It will be okay."

She wanted to say more but her cell phone started to ring. Recognizing the tune, she rolled her eyes and grabbed it from the counter. It was Joey, one of the college kids who helped part-time throughout spring, summer and fall. He was a great worker, people liked him, he rarely complained but he was one of those people who things just happened to.

A minute later, she disconnected and looked up and found Colby watching her over his coffee cup. "Flat tire." She grimaced. "I've gotta go pick him up. The jobs today will take twice as long if he isn't around."

"Still think you'll get done fairly early?" he asked, reaching out and catching her hand. His thumb stroked along the inside of her wrist as he lifted it up and pressed a kiss to her palm. He hadn't shaved and his roughened cheek rasped against her flesh.

"Should be. Why?"

He shrugged and tugged her to stand between his widespread thighs. He had one bare foot braced on the floor, the other on the rung of the stool. Wearing nothing but his jeans, he looked entirely too good to walk away from. His eyes were still heavy with sleep and the early morning sun filtering through the window did amazing things to his body. She found herself fantasizing about sliding her fingers through the hair on his chest, tugging just a little before she continued on downward and unzipped his jeans.

Fantasizing to the point that she was practically drooling and she hadn't heard a damn thing he'd said, she realized, jerking her eyes up to his face. A sexy smile curled his lips as she said dumbly, "Huh?"

"I was thinking maybe I could take you out tonight. Something nice."

"How nice?"

He grinned. "Nice as in I'm going to see if I can find a tie, maybe talk you into wearing a dress...and not wearing any panties."

Blood rushed to her cheeks. Heat curled in her belly. "How does me not wearing any panties have anything to do with how nice a place you take me to?"

He slid a hand between her thighs and cupped her, rubbing the heel of his palm against her. "Well, I don't guess it would be fair if I said I'd only take you out if you leave the panties off but it sure as hell would be fun for me to think about you being naked under some sexy black dress."

She cocked a brow at him, tried for a cool smile but ended up whimpering as he pressed his finger against her, pressing through the layers of her shorts and panties. "I think I can find something black and sexy. And panties are overrated."

He hauled her against him and kissed her, quick and rough. When he let go, they were both breathing hard and heavy. "Clothing is overrated, if you ask me. Especially considering how damn good you look without any."

* * * * *

Colby stood in the doorway, staring into the room.

It looked bare.

Over the past month, he'd slowly been getting rid of all of Alyssa's things. All of her clothes had been donated to a local church group. Other things, like books, her knick knacks, the fairies and dragons she'd collected had been boxed up and given to DAV.

All that remained in their room now was the furniture. A guy who worked for Bree was taking the bedroom set. He was coming over tomorrow to pick it all up and then the room would be empty.

It was hard, but not as hard as he'd expected. Instead of a driving grief, he'd been able to go through her things with a sad sort of acceptance. His wife was gone. In the past month, he hadn't even heard the whisper of her voice and he supposed it was because he had finally come around to accepting it—and getting back to some sort of life.

Life.

Yeah, he had a life again and it was actually looking a hell of a lot better than he could have expected. Better than he had even wanted, in all honesty.

He was falling in love with Bree. It was a slow, lazy drift, completely different from the way Alyssa had danced into his heart back when they were still kids.

But he'd mostly expected that. Everything with Bree was different.

The friendship that had always been between them had grown into something else and he could even admit, without feeling too guilty, some of it had started before he'd even left. The way she'd been there with Alyssa as she'd gotten more and more ill, the way she'd stood by him, a silent source of comfort during those last days. It had planted something inside him.

Falling in love again wasn't something he'd planned on.

Wasn't even something he'd wanted. The pain of losing somebody was enough to make most people leery, he guessed.

But it had crept up on him. Colby was a lot of things, but he wasn't a complete idiot. Life was giving him a second chance at happiness and he wasn't going to walk away from it.

Well, there were still a few unanswered questions there. Like how Bree felt, for one. He thought he knew, but he needed to know for sure. Needed to hear her say it. Tonight, he was going to see if he couldn't get her to do just that.

Slowly, he stepped into the room, staring at the bed. He'd shared this bed with Alyssa for years. He'd saved this part for last, determined to work his way up to it, but now he realized he hadn't needed to do that. He stripped the comforter away, folding it neatly and laying it in a box by the door. If the guy wanted the sheets and blankets, he was welcome to them, otherwise Colby would just drop them by DAV with the last of the books he still had to box up.

He stripped off the pillow cases, the top sheet, adding them to the box. Reaching under the mattress, he tugged the gathered corner of the bottom sheet. On Alyssa's side, near the top, he did the same. His fingers brushed against something. His heart skipped a beat as he grabbed it and pulled it out.

Her journal. He knew what it was even before he saw it. There was a box full of them up in the attic and that was one thing he had no idea what to do with. He couldn't just give her journals away, but throwing them out didn't seem right. One thing Alyssa had done faithfully was write in it almost every day. Even the day before she died, she'd written something in it. Granted, it took her forever to finish an entry but when he offered to write it down for her, she'd always refused.

He hadn't ever looked inside them but now, he found himself opening it, staring down at her familiar, flowery-looking script. Time ticked away from him as he read. The first entry was in February, the last one the day before she died. Most of what she wrote had his eyes burning. How she'd been so afraid most days, often angry. But the last few weeks were different. The entries were shorter, not quite as descriptive, but she'd been so weak that he understood why she didn't go into as much detail.

He reached the last entry, but before he started to read, he closed his eyes and tipped his head back. When he felt a little steadier, he started to read. But three lines in, he wished he hadn't.

Wished he had just thrown this journal in with the others or even in the garbage.

I got Colby to leave for a little while. Bree's on her way over and I need some privacy for this. Can't exactly have him lurking around while I ask this, right? I don't think he'd understand me telling her that I want her to hook up with him.

That was all he read.

All he needed to read.

Snapping it closed, he stood up and started for the door, rage churning inside him, a sick sense of betrayal threatening to drive him insane. Bree—

Fuck.

He stopped and looked down at the journal in his hand. Abruptly, he turned and hurled it across the room. It hit the wall and fell to the ground. He almost left it there. Almost. He stormed down the hall, torn between just leaving again and never coming back and finding Bree, demanding that she confess the truth. That the past month had been a fucking lie. She'd slept with him, spent time with him because it had been the final wish her best friend asked of her.

He was going to be sick.

But he stopped in his tracks, turned, went back and got the journal.

He had to see the look on her face when she read it, had to see how she reacted when he asked her to explain what in hell the past month had been about. He'd been falling in love with her.

She was fucking him out of some bizarre loyalty, maybe mixed with a little bit of pity.

What really sucked was that he almost could have handled the pity. He fell in love with a friend, no reason she couldn't do the same but he knew it wasn't pity that drove her. How far would she have let it go? How far did her loyalty to Alyssa go?

He didn't know the answer to that.

But he sure as hell was going to find out.

* * * * *

Sexy dress.

Check.

No panties.

Check.

Hair done.

Check...and she'd actually spent some time on it too.

Makeup.

Check.

Only thing missing was Colby.

Even after an hour had passed and he wasn't there, she wasn't worried. If she knew a damn thing about him, he was probably at the house, debating about the proposal he'd mentioned. She basically knew what one was and she also knew that he would drive himself crazy trying to get every last word exactly right. Which meant she just might need to go and get him, otherwise another two hours could pass before he bothered to check the time.

She got her purse, slid her feet into a pair of black heels and headed out. A breeze was blowing and she flushed as it blew the skirt of dress over her bare rump. She wasn't the type to go without panties and the feel of the air caressing her under the skirt was both discomfiting and erotic.

The drive to the house was quick. His car, that junky looking clunker he had yet to get rid of, was parked in front of the house. It was getting late but the only light on inside the house was the one in his office. With a grin, she shook her head and headed up the stairs. The front door was unlocked. She didn't bother knocking as she slipped inside and called his name.

No answer.

She frowned, pushed a hand through her hair, unconsciously messing up the style she'd spent nearly forty-five minutes on. Her heels clicked on the floor as she walked to the office. He was in there all right but he wasn't working. He was sitting at the desk. As she stepped inside, his gaze cut to her, his eyes hard and cold.

"Hey." Licking her lips, she took a few steps toward him, although something inside her whispered a warning.

He didn't say anything.

The black slip dress she wore seemed terribly inadequate now. She was cold, goose bumps roughing up her flesh. Her palms had gone damp and automatically, she smoothed them down her skirt. "Something wrong?"

In response, he tossed something he'd been holding onto his desk. Bree frowned, cocking her head. It was a journal, an embossed leather cover…recognition struck. Alyssa's journal. Bree had seen it at a street fair and bought a couple of them, one for herself, the other for her best friend's birthday. Bree's was at home, tucked inside her night stand, a few scattered entries, either from a really bad day when she just needed to vent or cry or rage, or a really good day that she just had to commit to paper.

Alyssa had been almost religious about her journal writing though.

Something cold settled in the pit of her belly as she picked up the journal.

"Interesting read." He finally spoke but he sounded nothing like himself. Too harsh. Too cold. Too brittle. "The last entry is a real eye-opener."

Bree tore her gaze from his face and opened the journal. Her fingers felt thick, awkward as she turned the pages, seeking out that last entry. It was dated the day before Alyssa had died.

The pit of her belly dropped as she read the first few lines.

I got Colby to leave for a little while. Bree's on her way over and I need some privacy for this. Can't exactly have him lurking around while I ask this, right? I don't think he'd understand me telling her that I want her to hook up with him.

"Colby..."

He stood up, stalked around the desk. Instinctively, she backed away, her hand falling to her side, the journal hanging from her fingers.

"So I guess me coming back made it a little easier for you to keep that promise."

Bree took a breath and said, "Colby, listen."

He shook his head. "Nothing really to listen to, is there? It's the truth, right? At first, I had to hear you admit it, but I can tell just by looking at you. So what have I been? Was it all for Alyssa? Did you ever feel a damn thing for me? Did I even rate a pity fuck or was it all for her?"

Colby stood close now, too close. The heat of his fury all but scalded her, yet she was still cold—cold to the core.

"She's dead, you know. She wouldn't have known if you kept the promise or not. I've gotta admire the loyalty, Bree, but don't you think you're taking friendship a little too far?"

Words—damn it, they were lodged in her throat. She could explain this. Hell, she understood why he was so pissed. She would be too. But he had it wrong—damn it, did he have it wrong. She swallowed the knot, tried to speak, even though her vocal cords felt frozen. "Loyalty doesn't have anything to do with this, Colby."

"Doesn't it? Your best friend is worried about her husband, pathetic shy bastard that he is, and she doesn't want him to be alone. So she just decides you'd make a good match, a nice little sacrificial lamb."

Narrowing her eyes, she snapped, "I'm not a lamb, pal. Sacrificial or otherwise. And you're not pathetic. You need to just chill out and listen to me—"

He reached out and hauled her against him, muffling her startled yelp with a hard, cruel kiss. Against her mouth, he rasped, "No, I just need to go ahead and just take whatever in the fuck you're giving me."

His hand fisted in her long skirt, jerked it up until he could palm the naked flesh of her ass. His thigh forced its way between hers and despite herself, despite her growing outrage, her body reacted. Heat boiled through her as he rubbed his jeans-clad leg against the mound of her sex.

If he hadn't said anything—but he did. And probably it was a good thing. His voice was a hard slap, jerking her back to reality, even as he reached between her thighs and cupped her, pushing two fingers into her wet pussy. "You really do commit yourself, don't you? You don't just hook up with me, you get wet when I touch you. You come and scream and beg for more. Way to get into it, sugar."

Recoiling, she tried to pull away from him. He spun them around, trapping her up against his desk. The wood felt cold under her bottom as he lifted her up onto it and stepped between her thighs. Bree shoved her hands against his chest. "Let me go, Colby."

"Why? Isn't this what you're supposed to be doing? Making me feel better? Comforting me? Taking care of me? Whatever in the fuck it was you agreed to?" he snarled, lifting his head just enough to glare down at her.

But when he would have crushed his mouth back to hers, she averted her head. He fisted a hand in the short strands of her hair, forced her mouth back to his. The taste of him, the feel of his body moving against hers—it was almost enough to drown out the voice screeching in the back of her head. Almost. He reached between them, the backs of his fingers brushing against her pussy as he unbuttoned his jeans and dragged the zipper down.

The rasping sound of it was unbelievably harsh—too harsh, too loud. Time slowed to a crawl, each second dragging out and lasting what seemed like forever. The temperature in the room dropped and even with the furnace-like heat his body threw off, Bree was freezing. Something whispered in her ear.

A voice. But it was indistinct, muffled—more like listening to somebody speaking in another room. It was surreal, surreal enough to drag her more completely back to herself and she jerked away as Colby shifted, pushing her thighs wider.

No.

She swallowed, reached up, unsure whether she was going to shove him away and pull him close. But he already owned so much of her. He had her heart, though she knew she couldn't ever tell him, not after this. He had her soul. But he'd never believe her.

She'd be damned if she let him claim her self-respect too.

Reaching deep, she found the strength of will to push against his chest as he pressed the head of his cock to the entrance of her body. He slid inside—just the first few inches—and as she locked her arms and shoved, he went still. His eyes glittered at her from under his lashes and somehow, behind the fury, she saw the pain. But she couldn't give in. If this happened—fuck, she was already destroyed—but if this happened, it was going to destroy him. She could forgive him. He'd never hurt her physically and she loved him enough to let him take whatever he needed from her and she'd give it freely.

But when his fury cooled, even if he still thought she was just acting out Alyssa's wishes, he'd look back at what had happened and he'd never forgive himself.

"Don't do this, Colby."

He reached up, caught one hand, dragged her wrist behind her back and stepped closer, forcing another inch of his rigid penis inside her vagina. Bree lowered her head and closed her eyes as he caught the other wrist. Before he could, she drew her hand down, stiffened it and struck, driving into the vulnerable flesh of his neck. He stumbled back, his face going red as he choked for air. Bree slid off the desk, keeping a wide berth as she circled him.

"Goodbye, Colby."

On legs that shook, she walked away from him. With hands that shook, she just barely managed to open the door to the house, the car. Climbing inside, she sat there, trembling all over. Tears burned her eyes, blinded her. Harsh sobs escaped her and the rush of blood pounding in her ears left her deaf to anything and everything else.

What had just happened?

*****

What had just happened?

Maybe it was the temporary lack of oxygen flowing to his brain, he didn't know. But he sat there on the floor, confused and sick inside. He rubbed his throat, swallowed against the pain there and sat on the floor with his back to his desk, mired in a pit of self-disgust.

What the hell had he almost done?

How could he have done that? Thought it? Anger, hurt, betrayal, none of it mattered, none of it was any excuse. Regardless of what had set him off, he'd just tried to force himself on Bree—a woman he'd fallen in love with.

He'd come this close to raping her—this close to crossing a line he hadn't thought he was capable of crossing. That he wouldn't have hurt her didn't matter because she'd told him to stop.

He hadn't been able to make himself do it. For a few minutes, he'd been incapable of it.

Even in the still-sane part of his brain, where he had watched what he was doing in disgust, completely appalled, he hadn't been able to find the strength to stop what he was doing.

She had done it.

He heard the deep rumble of the engine as she started the truck just outside his window. Clarity struck and he managed, just barely, to shove himself to his feet, out into the hall. His legs were stiff, not wanting to work for him. He knew she wouldn't want to see him, knew she wouldn't want to talk him. But he couldn't just let her drive off. He needed to tell her he was sorry—fuck, what a lousy word. Needed to make sure she was okay.

But before he even managed to get to the door, she had pulled off.

He watched through the glass pane as she drove away. What little strength he had drained out of him and he sank to the floor.

What the hell had he done?

Chapter Nine

She wouldn't return his phone calls.

She wouldn't talk to him.

She wouldn't answer the door the one time he made himself go over there.

Colby couldn't blame her, but even knowing she didn't want to see him, he wouldn't let himself take the coward's way out. He needed to face her and apologize—regardless of why she had been with him, he had no excuse, no reason for what he'd almost done.

The weight of the guilt returned in full force, but this time it had nothing to do with dreaming about a woman while his wife lay dead under six feet of earth. It had to do with the fact that he'd attacked the woman he loved and almost done something that would have scarred them both. Hell, he *was* scarred from it.

Never in his life had he ever lost control like that—never felt the threads of his temper unravel and drive him to do something unthinkable. Whatever mental punishment he could heap on himself, he deserved it.

That and so much worse.

But Bree… She didn't deserve what he'd almost done and he couldn't get her to look at him long enough for him to make some sort of apology. He'd even tried tracking her down at work but it was as though the guys who made up her crew had some kind of radar because they drew around her and the only way he was going to get to her to apologize would be if he fought his way through.

He was even tempted to do it. A couple of her crew were big-ass bastards who could probably lay him flat on the concrete, and getting his ass kicked was the least he deserved. But what he needed to say to her needed to be done in private. He just wished he could catch her alone for five minutes so he could crawl to her and tell her how fucking sorry he was.

"You have no idea how damn sorry you should be."

Colby closed his eyes. After four nights of sleeplessness, four days of hell on earth as he worried about Bree and relived every last moment of that night, the last thing he needed was a self-induced hallucination.

"I'm not a hallucination, you bastard. Look at me."

He opened his eyes and stared at his wife's face. She was livid. She was also a lot more transparent than normal. "It's because I'm livid, sugar. It takes concentration to make myself be seen and I'm so damn pissed off at you, it's taken this long just be able to focus enough to tell you how fucking pissed off I am."

"I don't need this," he rasped, shoving out of the chair in his office and lurching past her.

She had no intention of letting him escape so quickly, though.

"No, you either need to get your head examined or your eyes checked. Colby, are you blind? Do you really think Bree did a damn thing she didn't want?"

She appeared before him, just flat, outright appeared — no walking past him, circling around — just blink and there she was, hovering in front of him and looking a lot less substantial than she had before. Her eyes narrowed and she snapped, "Would you stop thinking like a fricking writer and just pay attention to me? Yeah, I'm less substantial because I'm not supposed to *be* here anymore. All I wanted, the only thing that kept me here, was needing to see you happy. Happy with her because you're the only damn person who will make her happy. I thought I'd done it, thought I was done here but then you had to go read that damn journal."

Glaring at her, he snapped, "That damn journal is the whole fucking problem. No, fuck that, that isn't the problem. The problem is that you couldn't just let things be. You had to go after Bree and ask her for something you had no right to ask."

"I asked her to go after the one person she's always wanted," Alyssa said, her voice thin, reedy, getting ever more distant. "You!"

Gruffly, he told her, "You don't know what the hell you're talking about."

"I'm talking about my best friend, and trust me, I damn well know what I'm talking about." Her voice wavered, thinned out, disappeared altogether and for a second, so did she, her misty form winking out.

A cold breeze shuddered through the room, followed by something that sounded like a sigh. Alyssa shimmered back into view, a pained look on her face. "I'm running out of time, Colby. If I don't cross over soon, I don't know if I'll be able to. I'll end up trapped and I don't want that. Will you shut up and listen to me?" Her head cocked, long curls spiraling over her shoulders. "You didn't read the last entry, did you?"

His mouth twisted. "That's the whole fucking problem, Lys. I did read it."

She cocked a brow and said, "Apparently not, not if you think Bree was with you for any reason other than the fact that she wanted to be." Her eyes closed and she shook her head. "Take another look, Colby. And stop being so blind."

Then she was gone.

And somehow, deep inside, he knew this time, it was for good.

"Goodbye, Lys," he whispered. Exhausted, depressed, he started toward his room.

But then he stopped and looked back at his office. The journal was still sitting on his desk, exactly where he had placed it the night Bree had walked away from him.

A muscle jerked in his jaw as he took it. Something vile and ugly pumped inside him but he made himself open it, made himself flip through to the last entry. Made himself face how damn foolish he'd been.

Take another look, Colby.

Alyssa's words echoed in his ears and he turned the next page, but it was blank. As was the next and the next…and the next. Disgusted, he started to flip back. Then, for some reason, instead of flipping back, he flipped forward, toward the end of the book.

And there it was. On the third to last page.

She told me. I could tell she didn't want to, but I guess Bree just couldn't lie to me. Part of me always knew that she loved him, but I never let myself think about it. How could I? My best friend in love with my husband. She acts so guilty, keeps apologizing like she's done something wrong, like she thought I suspected her of putting the moves on him.

I don't know. Maybe I'd feel the same. It can't be easy falling for the guy who marries your best friend. She kept telling me she couldn't do it, that Colby didn't want her like that. Not now, he doesn't, but I think he will. Maybe I should have just kept out of it, let whatever will happen just happen. I just hate to think about Colby being alone and I hate to think about her loving him like she always has but never doing anything about it.

She'll do what she can to help him but I don't know if she'll do what I asked her to. She just kept telling me 'no'. Man, I hope I didn't screw this up. I just want them to be happy.

That was it. Dated the day she died. Each word was successively fainter than the previous and by the time he read the last word, the print was so light and shaky, he had to squint just to make it out.

Carefully, he closed the journal. Just as carefully, he laid it aside and then he braced his hands on the desk, shoulders bowed forward. His head slumped and he stared downward but he wasn't seeing the journal, wasn't seeing the desk, wasn't seeing anything but Bree's face.

One memory after another flashed through his mind.

It was like a movie reel. The day of the funeral. The day Alyssa had sent him out for lime sherbet she could barely eat. The look on Bree's face when she crashed into him just outside the bedroom. How she looked when she saw him after he finally came back home. The careful, guarded way she held herself around him, as though she was hiding something.

Was she?

Shit.

Had Alyssa been right?

Is that what Bree kept hidden from him?

There was only one way to find out, but considering she didn't want to speak to him, didn't want to see him, probably wanted nothing to do with him, getting that answer wasn't going to be easy.

* * * * *

He didn't bother calling.

Didn't bother knocking.

In fact, he didn't even drive his car over to her house. He called a cab and paid the ridiculous fare just so he could use his key and let himself into her house while she was still working. If she saw his car, he wouldn't be surprised if she just drove right on past. So he just headed that possibility off.

This way, at least if she still didn't want to talk to him, she'd have to deal with him long enough to get him out of her house. Give him long enough to apologize…and hopefully get an answer to his question.

He settled in her library, sitting in an overstuffed armchair that smelled of flowers and Bree, with a full view of the driveway. He'd see when she drove up and hopefully, he'd have the time to prepare some sort of apology, some way to ask her what he needed to know.

Time was one thing he ended up having plenty of. He waited in her house for four hours. The hour hand on the clock kept ticking away and by the time she finally turned into the driveway, it was after eight. Belatedly, he remembered that she'd been contracted to the landscaping on the upscale subdivision up on the hill and the job had started this week.

The house was so quiet that he heard the garage door open, shoved out of the chair and moved to stand in the door to wait for her. With his hands jammed deep into his pockets, he rested his shoulder against the doorjamb. And waited.

When she came through the door, Colby's heart leapt into his throat, lodged there for a brief moment and then sank down somewhere in the vicinity of his knees. Knees that went just a little bit weak at the sight of her.

She looked exhausted, hauntingly fragile, with circles under her eyes that were so dark, they looked like bruises. Bree didn't notice him at first as she nudged the door shut behind her and dropped her keys and cell phone onto the counter just inside the door. She crossed the gleaming wooden floor, shambling to a halt in front of the refrigerator. Listless, she opened the door and just stood there, staring inside with absolutely no interest.

"I don't know about you but I haven't had much of an appetite all week," he said quietly.

Bree tensed.

The hand holding the door open went white in the knuckles but she didn't slam it shut and turn and rail at him to get the hell out of her house. Instead, she eased it closed and then turned around. She tucked her hands into her back pockets, the grass-green T-shirt she wore drawing tight across her breasts.

"What do you want?"

He shrugged restlessly. "A lot of things. Turning back the clock a week sounds like a good way to start. But that isn't going to happen. So first up, I guess I should tell you I'm sorry."

Her lashes lowered, shielding her eyes. "I figured that out after the first five messages you left on my machine. Okay. You're sorry."

"I wouldn't want to hurt you for my life."

She turned away, moving to stare out the window over the sink. The pool was visible from the window and staring at it sent a fresh lance of pain driving through him. It hadn't even been a month since he'd made love to her for the first time, right by the pool.

"I know that. And you didn't." She didn't look at him as she spoke, just stared outside.

With a derisive snort, he said, "Then apparently you weren't paying attention. That's exactly what I almost did."

"But you didn't. It's over. It's done. You've apologized. Now would you please leave?"

"That's not the only reason I'm here."

Now she finally looked at him, shooting him a narrow glance over her shoulder that managed to convey more than a thousand-page thesis. "I don't really care what other reasons you have for being here, Colby. You want to think I'm just sleeping with you because Alyssa wanted me to. Great opinion you have of me."

She stalked past him without another look. Making it pretty clear that she was done with the conversation. *Too damn bad,* Colby thought. Hell, he'd already fucked things up. He couldn't make it any worse, right?

So as she headed toward her room, he followed her and when she would have slammed the door in his face, he wedged his foot against it and bodily forced his way into the room.

Bree glared at him, her arms crossed over her breasts, foot tapping against the floor in an erratic rhythm. "You know, the Neanderthal bit just doesn't work for you."

"Do you love me?"

Her eyes widened. He could see the pulse slamming away under the fragile skin in her throat. "Wuh…what?"

"Do you love me?" he repeated, closing the distance between them.

She retreated from him but ended up backing herself against the wall. Colby kept his distance as he waited for her to answer him. Even though all he wanted was to reach for her and pull her close, hold her tight, never let go.

"Is that why the hell you barged your way into my room?" she asked, her voice caustic.

"Yes. You haven't answered me. Do you love me?"

Bree sneered at him. "Sex doesn't equal love, Colby. I realize that you hooking up with your high school sweetheart doesn't exactly make you an expert on the subject but you're not naïve. You know life doesn't work like that."

"I also know that you're not the type to fall into bed with any guy you meet." She wouldn't look at him, not directly. Over the past few weeks, up until he'd fucked up so badly, she'd lost some of the evasive caution she always showed around him. But now it was back. Back in full force and she wouldn't meet his eyes for anything.

He figured there could be a few reasons for that. The first one left him almost sick as he considered it, so he had to ask. "Are you afraid of me?"

Dark gray eyes narrowed and she shoved off the wall, advancing on him until the toes of her work books bumped his tennis shoes. "Afraid of you? Please," she scoffed.

Okay, so if she wasn't afraid of him…well, there was only one other option that made sense. Still, he wasn't quite sure he wanted to put any faith in that idea just yet. Slowly, he reached up, cupped her face. Dragging his thumb across her lower lip, he stared into her eyes, watched as her pupils spiked, flared until just a thin sliver of gray showed. "If you're not afraid of me, then why do you have such a hard time looking at me?"

"I'm looking at you right now," she pointed out.

"Then look at me and answer my question."

She batted at his hand and slipped away from him. "You're asking me a question you really don't have any right to ask."

That, in itself, was almost answer enough for him. Bree wasn't a coward. By nature, she wasn't the evasive type, unless it involved him. If she didn't love him, she'd flat out tell him. He took another step toward her and this time when she backed away, he didn't let it deter him. "I think I do have the right. But maybe I should tell you something first."

"The only thing you should do is just leave me alone."

As she tried to brush past him, he caught her arm, whirled her around until she crashed into his chest. Sliding his arms around her waist, he held her close. "Oh, you might be right on the money there. I *should* leave you alone and I've got no right to expect much of anything from you after the other night. But I need to know the answer." His hand slid up over her side, along her shoulder, curved along her neck. Using his thumb, he angled her chin up.

Her eyes were dark and stormy gray, her body rigid against his. He lowered his head, pressed his mouth to hers, but she remained unyielding.

"Why?" she demanded, averting her head. "What difference does it make?"

"All the difference in the world," he whispered against her cheek. He rubbed his mouth along the smooth, silken skin, then lifted his head to watch her face as he told her. "I love you, Bree. I love you, so your answer makes all the difference in the world."

Her mouth fell open. Tears gleamed in her eyes. A harsh breath rasped out of her and her body went slack in his arms. "You...what...what did you say?"

He'd been terrified to tell her, he realized. Absolutely terrified. But now, he wasn't entirely sure why. Cupping her chin in his hand, he lowered his mouth to hers and this time when he kissed her, she didn't pull away. "I love you," he said against her lips.

Her hands clutched at the front of his shirt, grasping handfuls of the worn cotton.

Lifting his head, he stared down at her, watched as a couple of tears broke free and slid down her cheeks. He licked them away.

The feel of his mouth on her had Bree shuddering. She wanted to grab onto him. Hold him close. Demand he say it again...and again...and again.

But what if he didn't mean it? Or what if he was wrong?

What if—

From the depths of her subconscious, another voice started to whisper. Alyssa's voice, or rather the memory of it. Something she'd said only a few short weeks ago. Yet in a way, it felt like another lifetime.

What if it means everything?

What ifs. What did they add up to? Too often heartbreak, headache, misery, confusion—regret.

Swallowing, she worked her fingers free from his shirt and pushed against his chest. He let go but she could tell he didn't want to. She had to think, though. And she couldn't think with him touching her. It just wasn't possible. Taking a few steps away, she turned her back on him and rubbed her hands over her face.

A minute to think. She needed just a minute—no. Maybe a little more time. A few days. Think it through, try to...oh, the hell with that.

Turning back to him, she asked, "Do you mean that?"

"If I didn't mean it, why the hell would I say it?"

Okay…good answer. Her head was spinning, her chest aching. It dawned on her that she really wasn't breathing a whole hell of a lot. Breathing. Needed to breathe. Sucking in a deep gulp of air, she waited for the room to quit spinning around on her. It didn't happen though and Bree realized it had nothing to do with her breathing or lack of. She stumbled, a little off balance and ended up bracing her hands on the back of the nearest chair. "You really mean it?"

His lips curved. That sexy, yummy mouth… Her heart skipped a beat as he took one step, then another toward her, staring at her with eyes that held heat and promises. "I mean it. I love you."

He cornered her up against the chair but this time, even if the thought occurred to her to move away, she doubted she could. Her legs weren't working much better than her lungs. "Really?" she whispered again. "As in…for real?"

Colby dipped his head and pressed his lips to hers.

She sagged in his arms as he murmured, "Really. As in *very* for real."

Bree wanted to cry. She wanted to laugh. She wanted to dance. And she wanted to find someplace quiet so she could sort all this out. But she couldn't move.

Well, that wasn't entirely accurate. She could move…some. She had no trouble sliding her arms around his neck and burying her face against him. "Really?"

A large hand slid around and cradled the back of her head, the other slipping around her waist and cuddling her close. "*Very* really."

Blindly, she turned her mouth to his and he met her kiss with a desperation that rivaled her own. Fisting her hands in his shirt, she jerked it upward, baring his chest but snarling in frustration when it got stuck under his arms. He leaned back and tore it off and then he did the same to hers. Her bra was next, torn away and left to fall to the ground.

Reaching for him, she groaned when he evaded her hands, focusing instead on the belt to her shorts. He stripped them away, knelt down to fight with her work boots while she braced her hands on his shoulders and tried to remain upright. The rest of his clothes, he didn't bother messing with, other than to tear open the fly of his jeans and shove both the denim and his boxers down.

When he pressed back against her, nothing separated them. He wrapped her in his arms and turned them, pressing her back to the wall. Bree lifted one leg, hooking it over his hip while he palmed her ass and pushed against her. She caught her lip between her teeth and whimpered as he entered her. Hard and thick, his cock stretched her, cleaving through her pussy with unrelenting force until he had buried himself inside her.

Colby reached down, hooked his arms under her knees, lifted her, opened her. She cried out, her lashes drifting down as waves of sensation threatened to swamp her. "No...don't close your eyes," he whispered, pressing his brow to hers. "I want to see you. I *need* to see you."

Dragging her lashes up, she stared into his eyes. He rolled his hips against hers, his movements slow and minute, as though he couldn't bear to pull too far away. She clenched down around him, her hands clutching at him, desperate to keep him close. Inside her pussy, he was rigid, blistering hot, scalding her — marking her.

He shifted his angle and when he rocked forward again, he brushed against her clit. Bree slammed her head back into the wall and cried out.

Against her neck, he muttered, "I love you."

"Colby," she pleaded, sliding her fingers into his hair. "Please..."

His cock throbbed, swelled, jerked. Sobbing, she rocked against him. He swore, his body tensing. The hands gripping her thighs tightened and for one second, he stilled within her. He shuddered and like a dam breaking, he exploded. His mouth covered hers, his tongue delving deep. He surged within her, falling into a hard, driving rhythm that had her screaming against his lips.

For the second time in his life, he knew he had totally lost control, but this time he didn't care. The need inside him no longer felt like some guilty secret he had to hide. What she felt for him was something real, not something born out of loyalty and promises—real. When she keened out his name, when her hands fisted in his hair and her body arched into his, it was real.

And even though she hadn't said it yet, he knew it. She did love him. He could taste it on her lips, feel in the way she moved against him, see in the dazed, stunned way she gazed at him as he told her. "I love you," he muttered again, lifting his head just long enough to tell her and see that stunned, shocked amazement dance across her face.

She came apart in his arms, her pussy clamping down on his cock and milking him, pulling him along with her. Burying his face against her neck, he climaxed with a groan. She shuddered against him, turned her mouth to meet his. Then she said it.

"I love you."

* * * * *

Alyssa couldn't see them very clearly now.

And she couldn't draw close, either.

It was like looking at them through a cloud and with every passing moment, it became harder and harder to see them.

It was for the best though.

A weight felt like it had dropped off her shoulders and she felt free.

She was done.

Done.

Behind her, something stroked her back, something warm, inviting. Slowly, she turned away from Bree and Colby and found herself staring at rays of light that chased away every last shadow.

It's time.

The words weren't spoken, but she felt them nonetheless.

A smile curled her lips and she nodded. *It's time.*

And without another look back, she moved toward the light.

Also by Shiloh Walker

A Hot Man Is the Best Revenge (Pocket)
All She Wants (Pocket)
A Wish, A Kiss, A Dream (*anthology*)
Belonging
Coming In Last
Djinn's Wish
Drastic Measures
Ellora's Cavemen: Legendary Tails II (*anthology*)
Ellora's Cavemen: Tales From the Temple IV (*anthology*)
Fated
Firewalkers: Dreamer
Firewalkers: Sage
Good Girls Don't
Hearts and Wishes
Her Best Friend's Lover
Her Wildest Dreams
His Christmas Cara
His Every Desire
Hot Spell
Love, Lies and Murder
Make Me Believe
Myth-behavin' (*anthology*)
Mythe & Magick
Mythe: Vampire

Nightstalker: Back From Hell
Once Upon a Midnight Blue
One Night with You
One of the Guys
Seasons of Magick *with Jennifer Dunne*
Silk Scarves and Seduction
Telling Tales
The Dragon's Warrior
The Dragon's Woman
The Hunters: Ben and Shadoe
The Hunters: Declan and Tori
The Hunters: Eli and Sarel
The Hunters: I'll Be Hunting You
The Hunters: Jonathan and Lori
The Hunters: Rafe and Sheila
Touch of Gypsy Fire
Voyeur
Whipped Cream and Handcuffs
Whispered Secrets

About the Author

Shiloh Walker has been writing since she was a kid. She fell in love with vampires with the book Bunnicula and has worked her way up to the more…ah…serious vampire stories. She loves reading and writing anything paranormal, anything fantasy, but most of all anything romantic. Once upon a time she worked as a nurse, but now she writes full time and lives with her family in the Midwest.

Shiloh welcomes comments from readers. You can find her website and email address on her author bio page at www.ellorascave.com.

Tell Us What You Think

We appreciate hearing reader opinions about our books. You can email us at Comments@EllorasCave.com.

Why an electronic book?

We live in the Information Age—an exciting time in the history of human civilization, in which technology rules supreme and continues to progress in leaps and bounds every minute of every day. For a multitude of reasons, more and more avid literary fans are opting to purchase e-books instead of paper books. The question from those not yet initiated into the world of electronic reading is simply: *Why?*

1. ***Price.*** An electronic title at Ellora's Cave Publishing and Cerridwen Press runs anywhere from 40% to 75% less than the cover price of the exact same title in paperback format. Why? Basic mathematics and cost. It is less expensive to publish an e-book (no paper and printing, no warehousing and shipping) than it is to publish a paperback, so the savings are passed along to the consumer.

2. ***Space.*** Running out of room in your house for your books? That is one worry you will never have with electronic books. For a low one-time cost, you can purchase a handheld device specifically designed for e-reading. Many e-readers have large, convenient screens for viewing. Better yet, hundreds of titles can be stored within your new library—on a single microchip. There are a variety of e-readers from different manufacturers. You can also read e-books on your PC or laptop computer. (Please note that Ellora's Cave does not endorse any specific brands.

You can check our websites at www.ellorascave.com or www.cerridwenpress.com for information we make available to new consumers.)

3. *Mobility.* Because your new e-library consists of only a microchip within a small, easily transportable e-reader, your entire cache of books can be taken with you wherever you go.

4. *Personal Viewing Preferences.* Are the words you are currently reading too small? Too large? Too… ANNOYING? Paperback books cannot be modified according to personal preferences, but e-books can.

5. *Instant Gratification.* Is it the middle of the night and all the bookstores near you are closed? Are you tired of waiting days, sometimes weeks, for bookstores to ship the novels you bought? Ellora's Cave Publishing sells instantaneous downloads twenty-four hours a day, seven days a week, every day of the year. Our webstore is never closed. Our e-book delivery system is 100% automated, meaning your order is filled as soon as you pay for it.

Those are a few of the top reasons why electronic books are replacing paperbacks for many avid readers.

As always, Ellora's Cave and Cerridwen Press welcome your questions and comments. We invite you to email us at Comments@ellorascave.com or write to us directly at Ellora's Cave Publishing Inc., 1056 Home Avenue, Akron, OH 44310-3502.

Cerridwen, the Celtic Goddess of wisdom, was the muse who brought inspiration to storytellers and those in the creative arts. Cerridwen Press encompasses the best and most innovative stories in all genres of today's fiction. Visit our site and discover the newest titles by talented authors who still get inspired - much like the ancient storytellers did, once upon a time.

Cerridwen Press
www.cerridwenpress.com

Discover for yourself why readers can't get enough of the multiple award-winning publisher

Ellora's Cave.

Whether you prefer e-books or paperbacks, be sure to visit EC on the web at www.ellorascave.com

for an erotic reading experience that will leave you breathless.

Made in the USA
Lexington, KY
28 July 2010